The
Earth Is Round

Margaret Epp

The Earth Is Round

Margaret Epp

Christian Light Publications, Inc.
Harrisonburg, VA 22801

THE EARTH IS ROUND

Christian Light Publications, Inc.,
Harrisonburg, Virginia 22802
© 1998 by Christian Light Publications, Inc.
All rights reserved. Published 1998
Printed in the United States of America

10 09 08 07 06 05 04 03 02 01   6 5 4 3 2

Originally published in 1974 by Kindred Press

ISBN: 0-87813-575-8

ACKNOWLEDGEMENTS

To the Board of Publications of the Canadian Conference of the Mennonite Brethren Church and to Dr. H. T. Huebert, who sparked the production of this book—To William Schroeder who generously gave me free use of his publication on the Bergthalers of Russia and Manitoba—To Steve Prystupa of the Manitoba Museum of Man and Nature—To J. C. Reimer and the Mennonite Village Museum at Steinbach—To Dorothy Huebert, delightful hostess and selfless chauffeur—To Susan Hiebert, fellow writer, under whose guidance I got my first closeup of the West and East Reserves—To Helena Dueck, hostess and efficient secretary, who did marvels of compact planning so my week in Steinbach yielded the utmost benefit to an enquiring writer—To all the cheerful senior citizens who shared with me not only their own reminiscences but those of their parents and grandparents, and so helped to recreate the vanished era for me—To all the fine and generous people my most grateful thanks. It's been said before, but never with more truth: Without your help this book could never have been written. I trust you'll find the results worthy of the combined efforts.

Margaret Epp
July, 1974

ABOUT THE AUTHOR

Miss Margaret Epp was born near Waldheim, Saskatchewan, but then accompanied her missionary parents to China at the age of two and one-half. For health reasons it was not possible to return to China for a second missionary term, so the family settled on a farm near Waldheim. Miss Epp attended a small country school, then took high school by correspondence. She graduated from Bethany Bible Institute at Hepburn, Saskatchewan, and took one year of training at Prairie Bible Institute. In 1945 she joined the staff at Bethany as Dean of Women, and instructor in English and history.

Miss Epp knew from the age of seven that she wanted to be a writer. In 1949 she began writing full time. *The Earth is Round* was the thirty-third book she had published in 19 years. She wrote many children's books, including *Prairie Princess, The Princess and the Pelican,* and *The Princess Rides a Panther. This Mountain Is Mine* and *But God Hath Chosen* are missionary biographies. *Walk in My Woods* gives an insight into her own life.

She had 39 books published altogether.

In addition, she wrote extensively for about 20 periodicals. Many of her books were published in hardcover editions, a number were serialized (up to five times) for magazines, and several were translated into German.

From her home in Waldheim, Miss Epp's research and assignments took her to many parts of the world.

CONTENTS

MAPS AND ILLUSTRATIONS

I
Excitement in Schoenthal

Afterwards Cornelia Harms thought how fortunate it was that the carriage hadn't arrived earlier. Even a few *minutes* earlier. It had been hard enough today to sit still in school, knowing what she knew. The carriage from the Molotschna colony was expected at any time now! A few minutes earlier, and she would have been in the middle of reciting the Psalm for the week. And she couldn't have finished. Excitement and curiosity would have chased every other thought from her mind.

Cornelia's father, Peter Harms, the Schoenthal village school-teacher, wasn't a harsh man. But he was strict. And at times Cornelia suspected that he was just a bit more strict with his own children than with the rest. Perhaps he had to be.

Not with Bernhard. *He* was born good. He couldn't help it. And there were times when Cornelia thought she really ought to hate him for it. Instead, she wasn't entirely sure that she didn't love him most of all in this world. Better at times than Mother and Father. Better any day than her big sister Agatha. Even if Agatha *was* going to be a fine lady, and live in a big house with many servants. Even if it was for Agatha's sake that the carriage was coming all the way from Molotschna, about 90 *Wersts* (60 miles) west, as soon as school had closed (today was the final day!) and Mother could get the packing done.

The trouble with Agatha was that she was grown up.

Ever since last year when she visited Aunt Gerda for a month, she was changed. Excited. Proud. Bossy.

Bernhard was gentle, obedient, and friendly, and studious. At 13 he was one of the older boys in school, though he didn't look it. He was a Harms, after all. Dark and slender and not very tall. Like Father. Like Cornelia herself. But not like her in temperament.

Across the schoolroom he gave her a smile when she finished the Psalm without a single mistake. She drew a relieved breath. Then the school rose to stand while Father read a prayer. Then they sang the closing hymn. And school was over until next November.

That was when the carriage arrived.

All of Schoenthal must have noticed it coming. It swept along the wide street that cut through the village from end to end. Children, dawdling home from school, scattered at its approach. Cornelia, standing on the house porch, could see them backed up against the picket fences, jumping up and down in their excitement, bug-eyed, staring. Everybody could see at first glance that this was no common vehicle.

There was dust and sweat on the horses, dust on the close-drawn curtains. The carriage had come a great distance. But the horses still had plenty of life left. They tossed their manes, snorting, and their hooves came tap-tapping down the street. The coachman used his whip, but only to add to the general noise and gaiety. The echo of its sharp crack went rattling away through all the treetops of the village.

Then, in the heart of the village, the horses swung smartly onto the little school yard. They drew up before the plain looking housedoor.

"Pr-r-r-r-r!" called the coachman.

Obediently his horses stood, heads up, like statues. But their nostrils were blowing in and out gently, and their dusty flanks heaved too.

Out of the house spilled two solid blond-headed boys, Cornelia's little brothers Johann and Anton. Behind them came the schoolmaster himself. He and the coachman conversed in Russian. Cornelia could understand some of it. She could guess the rest. She knew all the arrangements that had been made.

Next door to the village school lived the most important man in the whole Bergthal colony, the *Oberschulze*. He could do just about anything! He collected taxes. He settled quarrels. He saw to it that roads and bridges were built and maintained. He watched out to make sure that all grownups went to church regularly. If there was a drunkard in the village—watch out! The *Oberschulze* would get him! If there was a mother who was sloppy and lazy—well, just let the *Oberschulze* hear about it! It was his job to see to it that her house got cleaned up. That was how important he was.

He hired the school teacher, too, and it was through the *Oberschulze*, Jakob Penner, that the Peter Harms family moved to Schoenthal from the Molotschna colony five years ago. Cornelia, who was six then, could remember it well.

When the school teacher knew that the carriage would be coming all the way from Molotschna, he naturally went to his friend the *Oberschulze* for advice. All the farmers who lived in Schoenthal had large barns attached to the rear of their homes. There was a passageway separating the house from the barn, but in winter there was no need to step out into the cold at all in order to tend to one's horses and cows. It was safer this way, too. Thieves stole too many horses if the barn was a distance from the house.

The schoolmaster had no horses to guard. He had only one cow. It was stabled in a small shed that was attached to the teacherage, just as the teacherage was attached to the rear of the schoolhouse. The cowshed was no place for a splendid team of horses from the Molotschna! And wherever would the coachman sleep?

"No problem. No problem," rumbled Jakob Penner. He was a big man with a big voice. "There is plenty of room in my barn for the horses. And naturally the coachman will want to remain nearby. He can sleep with my outdoor servants."

So all the arrangements had been made. Father swung himself up to sit beside the coachman now, to act as guide.

"Hoa! Hoa!" called the coachman. The horses leaned forward, and again all Schoenthal treetops rattled with the echoes of the cracking whip. And now came the village boys. They came in troops, tearing past the school, Cornelia's brothers pelting at their heels. Behind them Cornelia could see some of the village fathers, walking faster than they usually did. Everyone, everyone was part of the excitement. Except she. And Bernhard of course. But even he was disappearing through the garden gate at that moment.

Cornelia considered following. She could cut across the teacherage garden, run through the large Penner garden, and there she'd be! But just then there came a sharp rat-tat-tat on the nearest window pane. Mother was there, peering through the curtain. She smiled, frowned, and shook her head, making urgent motions. They said,

That's no place for girls. Come. I want you indoors right away.

Cornelia sighed impatiently. *Why* did girls always have to miss the fun?

She had not noticed that the air outdoors was chilly. The moment she stepped into the warm kitchen, a long pleasurable shiver shook her from head to foot. It was shadowy in here. Almost lamp-lighting time now. And just about supper time, too. Cornelia sniffed. Something good was cooking in the kettle on the brick stove. Cornelia peered into the Big Room. No one there. Nothing but the grandfather clock that went ticking and tocking gravely to itself. Where had Mother disappeared to so quickly?

"Mahm!" called Cornelia, then held her breath, listening.

"Here. I am upstairs." Faintly the words drifted down.

Cornelia darted into the dark little passage that separated the teacherage from the cowshed. Stairs led upward here, and lamplight glowed on the rafters overhead. Cornelia ran up to poke her head over the edge of the floor.

This loft was a place of shadows and smells. Her nose quivered. Coal oil. That came from the lamp which sat on the floor. It threw shadows on the raftered ceiling, fearsome shadows that moved mysteriously. But of course, they were thrown by Mother and Agatha who were stooping over an old chest, emptying it. The chest would be travelling to the Molotschna with Agatha.

So there was this smell of old clothes that had been packed away for a long while. And leather. That came from the heap of old shoes. And smoke. That was from the ham and bacon that hung from the rafters. The dry dusty smell came from the mounds of grain that were

13

stored up here. And the strong bitter smell came from the cabbages and the strings of onions. It was funny how each thing smelled like itself and nothing else. You could mix the smells together, yet each remained separate. It wasn't like a soup. Chicken borscht, for instance. There each thing added to the flavor, but after it was cooked, nothing tasted just like itself any more. Not the meat, nor the cabbage, nor the potatoes, nor the tomatoes.

The thought of food made Cornelia hungry.

"It looks shabby, dreadfully shabby," she heard Agatha say discontentedly, looking at the chest. "It almost makes one ashamed."

"Ashamed? Of your father, perhaps, for not providing a better one?" said Mother quietly.

"Oh, no! I didn't mean— I know, of course, that Father is always busy in winter, teaching school. He doesn't have time to carve furniture as the other fathers do for their daughters. But is *is* a bit hard to go to my new home, and have all the servants see *that*." She pointed at it with one scornful foot.

That Agatha. She is a proud one, thought Cornelia. "Shall I set the table for supper, Mother?" she asked aloud.

"Yes. We're having bean soup," called Mother. Then she was speaking to Agatha again. "What's inside the chest, that is what really matters. And your father and I, we have tried our best to give you a good *Utstia* (dowry). Nice things for your new home."

Mother's voice was still quiet, but it shook a bit. Cornelia skimmed down the stairs noiselessly, gave the door a soft firm shove, then ran into the kitchen.

She hoped Father and the boys would come home soon. She was getting to be very hungry. She brought the big stoneware soupbowl from the pantry. And the pail that was jammed full of knives and forks and spoons. She brought soup plates for herself and Johann and Anton. They were considered too young to eat from the family bowl. She brought the dish of butter, and the large loaf of brown bread. And the large butcher knife. She sharpened it on the rim of the soupbowl, but she did not attempt to cut the bread. Once she had tried it. She still had a jagged scar on her left thumb to show for it.

Her work done, Cornelia propped her elbows on the table and began rocking backward and forward as she sank into deep thoughts—a pool of thoughts. About last year. About Agatha's visit to Aunt Gerda's place. About Wilhelm Franz who was soon going to be Cornelia's brother-in-law.

He was the son of a rich man. But all the same, his father had been Father's best friend when both of them were young schoolboys. When Gerhard Franz, Wilhelm's father, finished the village school in the Molotschna village, he wanted to go to Prussia for more study. He hoped to become a teacher. But his parents did not want him to go alone. They offered to pay the expenses if Peter Harms would travel with him and live and study with him. So both of them went away to attend further school and then university.

When Gerhard's older brother died, his parents called Gerhard home. There was no thought now that he could become a teacher, they said. He had to take the place of his brother, and learn how to manage the family estate. But still the friends remained friends. Once, Cornelia remembered, shortly before they came to Schoenthal to live, their whole family visited the Franz place for a day. It seemed like a palace! Enormous! There were acres of fields all around. There were servants everywhere. There was a huge orchard, and a large mill. There were rows of beehives, and many flower beds, and a large herd of cows. She remembered these things. But she also remembered Wilhelm. He teased Agatha, who was thirteen. He teased her until she cried, she was so angry with him!

Well, she wasn't crying over Wilhelm now!

After her visit to Aunt Gerda's place, Agatha came home with red cheeks and sparkling eyes. She was the prettiest she had ever been. She didn't even mention Wilhelm—unless she did so in private to Mother and Father. Once or twice Cornelia got suspicious that something strange was happening. She heard Mother and Agatha whispering and laughing softly. If it had been winter time she would have suspected they were sharing Christmas secrets. But this was in June.

Soon after, a letter arrived for Father from Gerhard Franz. He read the letter silently at the supper table, and his eyes twinkled across at Agatha every little while. Then he cleared his throat and read the letter aloud so the whole family might hear:

"My dear friend Peter, I wish you all the best. I write to inform you that our son Wilhelm is earnestly in love with your beautiful daughter, Agatha. That is the way it goes with young people, not? Wilhelm has opened his heart to his parents, and I write to ask if you would have any objections to their union. We, his mother and I, would be glad to welcome your daughter to our home and our hearts. If you and your wife, Sarah, are of the same mind, our son would like to come and visit you soon. You could talk over the rest of the affair then. I know you will write soon, so that our Wilhelm will not need to wait in anxious uncertainty any longer than is necessary.

Remaining as ever, your old comrade and true friend, Gerhard Franz."

Father teased Agatha by pretending that he and Mother would say no to Wilhelm. And Agatha became anxious, her eyes flashing, as she talked excitedly about what a good man Wilhelm was, and what a good home he wanted to give her. She got excited easily. Everybody was laughing, because all of them knew that Father was joking.

So an answering letter was written, and after a few weeks Wilhelm came. Not with a beautiful carriage and dashing horses, but on horseback, arriving after dark. Only a few people in Schoenthal ever found out that he had been there at all.

At first Cornelia felt shy toward him. Perhaps he felt a bit shy too. But he and Agatha went into the Big Room with Father and Mother, and they closed the doors. Bernhard winked at Cornelia as they washed the supper dishes together. It had seemed strange to see a rich man sitting down at the table with them, just like anybody. Well, he came out of the Big Room with a big smile on his face, and before the evening was over he was teasing Cornelia and Johann and Anton. As if he had known them always.

Not Agatha though. He looked at her as though she might be something good enough to eat. And as soon as he had left quietly for Molotschna again, Mother and Agatha got busy making pillows, and crocheting lace for pillow slip edgings, and knitting white stockings, and—

"Well, Cornelia!" Mother's voice startled Cornelia so

much that one elbow slipped from the table edge and she slammed her chin against the soupbowl!

"Alone in the dark, child?" added Mother. The lamp had come in with her and Agatha. "What are you doing here alone?"

"Thinking," said Cornelia, rubbing her chin.

That minute a horn sounded on the street.

"There come the cows," remarked Mother.

"May I milk Brindle today?" asked Cornelia eagerly. Agatha wouldn't mind, she was sure. Milking was one of the jobs that *Frau Wilhelm Franz* would never, never have to do. She'd just as soon begin not doing it now. Usually, this last while, Father did it, night and morning. But tonight he still hadn't returned from the Penner place.

The western sky was rosy red, and in its light you could see the village herd come parading down the main street. In the still air you could hear their hocks creaking. Each morning at seven, now that winter was gone, the cowherd sounded his horn at the end of the village street. Each household had to be through milking by then—or they had to bring the cows to the pasture later, and that was considered a great disgrace. At every farmstead gate, more and more cattle joined the herd. All day they grazed under the watchful eye of the herdsman.

At sunset matters were reversed. Farmstead by farmstead the herd dwindled. The cows never needed to be reminded where they belonged. Cornelia, waiting at the picket gate now, could see Brindle edging nearer. Other cows and their calves gave way so she could turn in at the schoolyard gate. This was where she belonged.

Nor did Cornelia need any light in the shed, except for the glimmer that came through the open door. Going

18

mostly by feel, she fastened Brindle in place, got the milkstool, and sat down to grip the pail between her knees. Her hands felt for the front teats. Soft, and long, and bulging. You squeezed with a rolling motion, taking care not to dig your fingernails into the soft flesh. Brindle had a swift, effective kick if you forgot. Once she knocked Cornelia down, along with the stool, and drenched her with milk for good measure.

But either Brindle was learning patience, or Cornelia was learning to do the job well. Her forehead rested against the smooth warm flank. Her ears heard the steady *strip-strop, strip-strop* sound. Her thoughts were mostly elsewhere, busy with a puzzle.

It concerned Agatha. Why was she so different? Especially toward Mother. Sort of snippy, like about the chest upstairs. *Was it because Mother was her step-mother and not her own mother at all?*

It seemed strange to think of it, but Father was married twice. His first wife was named Agatha Fehdrau. Which was how Agatha got her name. When that mother died, Father married her dearest friend, and her name was Sarah Siemens.

Stepmother is not a nice word, thought Cornelia. In so many stories stepmothers were horrid creatures. And it seemed as if this must be *true*. One of the girls in school, Lena Schultz, had a stepmother. She lived at the outskirts of Schoenthal. The stepmother would not allow her to come home for dinner at noon, the way her own children did. Each schoolday Lena carried her lunch, a piece of hard *Gruffbrodt* (brown bread), tied in her handkerchief. There were horrible whispered stories about how she got whipped for nothing at all, and almost starved, and how hard she was made to work. Cornelia

19

told her father, hoping he would say it wasn't true and for her not to listen. Instead, he looked dreadfully sad.

After that, once a week, he invited Lena to have dinner with the Harms family. Mother always made sure to have something especially good that day. Fried sausages, maybe, with *Kielke* (noodles). Or large thin pancakes. Or *Pluma Moos* (fruit soup) and boiled ham. Or *Fettkuchen.* (fritters.)

Once, when she came, her legs were covered with bloody stripes. Mother washed them and rubbed butter into the cuts. Her hands and voice were gentle, but her face was white. And after dinner, when Lena had gone, Cornelia heard her Mother say, "Now it is enough! Now it is time somebody interferes! This day I go to the *Oberschulze.* On Sundays Mrs. Schultz can sit in church, looking pious, and at home she can do this to her child."

"Her stepchild," said Agatha.

"Does it make any difference?"

"She doesn't treat her own children that way."

"To teach your children how to be cruel, that is the most cruel thing you can do! Those children are more to be pitied even than Lena!" Mother's eyes flashed when she said it. She could never be the cruel kind of stepmother. Never. She—

A gleam of lamplight shone into the cowshed, breaking into Cornelia's thinking. A voice called, "Almost through? Supper's waiting. *Everybody's* waiting."

After that Cornelia finished her job with a rush. Agatha was waiting to strain the milk into a milkpan in the pantry. Cornelia washed her hands quickly. After the family gathered around the table, Father read a chapter from the Bible. Then they stood for prayer and Father prayed aloud. Schoenthal did not believe in praying

20

TYPICAL MENNONITE
FARM IN RUSSIA ALSO
IN MANITOBA

V.FRIESEN

aloud, unless you read your prayer out of a book, but here at home, Father talked simply to God as if he might be talking to a dear friend.

"Well, Mother," he said when they took their seats again, "how soon can you be ready to leave for Molotschna?"

Mother ladled soup into the soupplates for Anton, Johann, and Cornelia. "Today is Friday . . . ." she said. "Saturday . . . . Monday . . . . By Tuesday morning, I think."

"No sooner?"

"Well, I have to prepare enough food for the journey—"

"No, not that," contradicted Father, beaming. "It is all planned. All ready. My old friend, Gerhard Franz, has arranged for each stop on the way. How far we are to travel each day, and where we are to spend our nights—at the big estates along the way. It is all arranged. Because the carriage will be loaded, and cannot go fast, there might be danger from bandits, so there will be two servants riding along with us. That too is arranged. Agatha, you are getting a kind and thoughtful father-in-law."

Cornelia dug her spoon into her soup and brought up a heaping spoonful of hot white beans. She blew on them softly.

Monday, she thought. Monday we leave for the Molotschna colony.

That was where all the Harms family members were born. Even Anton, who was a tiny baby when they made the move to Schoenthal. Cornelia remembered holding him now and then on the long trek. She remembered they had had a sale before leaving Molotschna. And after the sale they had lived with Aunt Gerda for a long while. At least, it seemed a long while.

Aunt Gerda's husband was Uncle Johann Siemens, Mother's brother. But Aunt Gerda herself used to be Gerda Fehdrau, and she was the sister of Father's first wife. So Agatha was her very own niece. They were good friends too. Agatha knew how to behave just the way Aunt Gerda liked to have her nieces behave.

But Cornelia— Well, what she remembered chiefly was all the don'ts that made you feel in everybody's way. *Don't slam the doors. Don't run in the garden. You'll break the stems of the flowers— There, what did I tell you! Don't chase the calves. You'll scare them. Don't go wading in the pond. You'll upset the ducks and geese, and dirty your clothes.— There, what did I tell you! My Martha never behaves like this when your Cornelia isn't here to lead her into mischief.*

Remembering that time, Cornelia asked cautiously now, "But where will we stay when we get to Molotschna colony?"

"At Aunt Gerda's and Uncle Johann's," said Mother.

"*Ach weh!*" (oh, dear!)

"Have you swallowed a sour cucumber?" asked Father, and everybody burst out laughing. Even Bernhard, which seemed unkind. But Mother said, "Cornelia is five years older now. Five years will have made a big difference. You'll see."

"*Martha* is a *very* ladylike girl," remarked Agatha.

Nobody said, "Well, so is Cornelia." Not even Mother.

She turned to Father, changing the subject. "Will you be looking for a teaching position in the Molotschna?"

Father finished buttering a large slice of moist rye

bread. He cut it in half, and gave one each to Johann and Anton.

"Well?" Mother was watching him expectantly.

"Penner wants me to stay here and teach another winter. Maybe that will be the last winter for Schoenthal." Father spoke quietly. But his eyes shone with excitement.

Cornelia, everybody, knew what he was thinking about. This spring, 1873, twelve men were travelling far across the ocean. They were going to a land called North America. Just like the twelve spies in the Bible! They came from the Old Colony, from the Molotschna, from Bergthal, from the Crimea— from every place in Russia where Mennonites lived. They had gone to look for new places to live, in new countries. Cornelia couldn't understand all the reasons why. It had something to do with the Czar. Something about a broken promise.

In school the boys and girls talked a lot about it. And when the men of the village gathered for a *Schulzenbott* (village business meeting) Father would have long conversations with Mother later, about who said what, and how the villagers felt about the question.

Actually, he didn't really belong on the *Schulzenbott*. He had no right to vote. He owned no land. Only landowners were allowed to cast a ballot. But he could write beautifully, so he was the village secretary. That was how he got to hear all the news.

"If reports are favorable from the other side," said Father, "it could be that the whole Bergthal colony will be going."

"How many people is that?" Bernhard drew the bowl of his spoon carefully across the edge of the family bowl. A sign that you were growing up was ·that you were able

24

to eat from the family bowl without dripping. Bernhard was a very tidy eater. There were no drips between him and the bowl.

"How many?" repeated Father, consideringly. "About three thousand."

Three thousand people moving away together, to make new homes in a new country! Three thousand crossing the ocean together!

"I hear there's a stirring in other colonies, too," said Father. "What would you say—" He carried a spoonful of soup to his mouth, chewed briefly, and swallowed. "What would you say if the Harms family would go too?"

For a moment there was a stunned silence.

"To America?" said Bernhard, his dark eyes sparkling.

"To *America*?" protested Agatha. "So far away from *me*?"

"How far is that?" Anton wanted to know. "As far as the Molotschna?"

"Much, much farther," said Mother, sounding absent-minded. "Don't swallow so fast. Chew your food before swallowing it."

"How far?"

"It's on the other side of the world."

"Ohm Schellenberg says there isn't any other side," nine-year-old Johann said, and bit a careful half-moon out of his slice of bread. With a bulging cheek he finished, "He says the world is flat."

"He says—" Bernhard took up the story, laughing, "he says that no one in the world has ever gone west, and kept going west, and come back from the east. He says if we're not careful we'll go too near the edge, and fall off."

Bernhard had to laugh so much that he got one of his

bad coughing spells. They always left him completely exhausted. When he could breathe easily again, Mother said soberly, "Now eat, all of you. No more talk."

Later Cornelia sat on the floor in the dark in the Big Room. Her back leaned against the brick heater that was built into the wall. This corner of the room was warm and cosy. Because she had milked the cow she did not need to help with the dishes. Agatha was doing them. Mother and Father came into the Big Room, but Mother didn't light a lamp. They sat down in their favorite rocking chairs. The chairs creaked. The grandfather clock tick-tocked. Mother's knitting needles clicked softly. For a while nobody said a word.

Then Mother spoke. "*Why*, Peter?" Her voice was pleading. She didn't have to explain what she meant. It was as though they could read each other's thoughts.

"Why not?" said Father.

"You have your work in Russia. We have all our relatives here. Do you think any of them will move? No, they are too comfortable."

"It's not a question of comfort, Sarah. You know that. Many are giving up comfort for the sake of their consciences."

"But you, Peter. Is it because of land hunger you are thinking of going? Is that it?"

Creak-creak went the rockers. *Tick . . . . tock . . . . tick . . . . tock . . . .* went the clock.

"Maybe," said Father. "Maybe. Partly. The Bible says that if a father does not provide for his own household he is worse than a heathen. And in Canada every man gets 160 acres of land, free. Think of that! I would have something to leave my family when I die."

26

"Peter!"

From the corner came a timid voice. "Should I— should I go away?"

"Aha, have we a little listener? Come here, Cornelia."

She scrambled to her feet. This was her father calling, not her teacher. She came unafraid.

"What advice would you give? Should we go to the new world too?"

"Not if Mother doesn't want to."

"Hear that, Mother? I promise, Cornelia, that if we go it will be only when your mother is completely willing."

Visitors came then. Neighbors did not knock on one another's doors. They simply walked in. Peter and Sarah Harms rose to greet their guests, the *Oberschulze* and his wife, and Ohm Schellenberg and his chubby little wife. There would be lively arguments tonight. The *Oberschulze* believed the earth to be round.

Cornelia shook hands dutifully with the guests, and she carried the coats of the women to the Middle Room, her parents' bedroom. The women had come to see Agatha's *Utstia*— all the things she and Mother had been busy at for almost a year now. They teased her about Wilhelm Franz. The news had spread fast today. Cornelia's brothers had disappeared into the Summer Room, their bedroom. Mother and her visitors sat down in the kitchen. Cornelia would have liked to listen to the men talking. Father was telling the story about his friendship with Gerhard Franz all over again. That was much more interesting than hearing Agatha tell how many shirts she and Mother had sewn for her chest, and how many pairs of stockings they had knitted.

In two more days she would be on her way to get married. It seemed very strange, suddenly, to think that she might never come back here. And if the Harms family moved to America—why, they might never see Agatha again!

But to think of owning 160 acres of land! Only well-to-do people had that much land in Russia.

II
A Stepmother—and a Bride

Near sunset on Wednesday evening the Harmses entered Steinfeld. It belonged to the Molotschna colony, and it was here that all of them were born. So, actually, they were coming home. But Cornelia's thumping heart didn't feel any home feeling at all.

"We've not met a single robber on the way," remarked Father thankfully.

"Too bad," said Johann.

"You'd be the first to be afraid if we really met one," said Cornelia with a sniff.

"I wouldn't."

"You would."

"No, I wouldn't."

"Yes, you would."

"I wouldn't . . . I wouldn't . . . I wouldn't . . . I wouldn't . . ."

"You would . . . you would . . . you would . . . you would . . ."

They might have kept up their race of *would* and *wouldn't* till both of them were breathless, but Father said hush, so they hushed. It was just as well. Cornelia really didn't feel cheerful enough for a good argument. As for Agatha, she wasn't talking at all. Her cheeks were like wild roses, and her eyes had that Wilhelm Franz look. Wilhelm's family was going to be at Aunt Gerda's for supper. It was going to be like an engagement party for the Franz and Harms families.

29

The horses seemed to have caught Cornelia's mood. They certainly were not dashing along the way they did when entering Schoenthal a few days ago. They had been well fed along the way at the big country estates where the Harmses spent their nights. But pulling a family— and a bridal chest—for ninety *wersts* was a heavy job. The chest was strapped to the roof of the carriage. Each night a guard had watched to make sure no thieves broke into it. And now, soon, it would go to where it belonged. Along with Agatha into Wilhelm's home.

The horses were trotting quietly toward the village mainstreet when the coachman suddenly called, "Pr-r-r-r-r!" The children popped out their heads to see why they were stopping.

There, down the village street, came the village herd of cows. A forest of horns twinkled in the late sunlight. Just as in Schoenthal. The herd was bigger, of course, and Father said the cows were a better grade too. Steinfeld was a rich village compared to Schoenthal.

But Cornelia thought wistfully that she missed the large hill in the Bergthal colony. The Bodena river flowed gently along the foot of the hill, and the river and the hill were the loveliest places for play in summer and for school outings. Already Cornelia's main feeling was one of lonesomeness for home. Perhaps the rather daunting prospect of meeting Aunt Gerda had something to do with this.

When the herd had passed the corner, losing more and more cows as it moved along, the carriage set in motion again. Nearer. Every moment they were coming nearer to the Siemens' farmstead.

"There's Uncle Johann's place!" exclaimed Agatha. *She* wasn't wishing for a sight of Schoenthal just then.

"And so this is Cornelia," said Aunt Gerda a few moments later.

Cornelia looked at her in silent astonishment. *Why, she's not as big as Mother! I always thought she was huge. It must be her big voice and her way of talking.*

"Not very big for your age," pronounced Aunt Gerda. "A true Harms. You could be two years younger than my Martha. She is milking cows now. She is a big help."

The Johann Siemens' house was large but tonight it was a confusing place, crowded with people. Cornelia could not sort them out properly. Which of the big boys were her cousins, and which were Wilhelm's brothers? If only everybody didn't talk so loudly!

Father and his "old comrade and true friend" were in one corner of the Big Room, talking over old times. They laughed a good deal, and must have been reminding one another of schoolboy pranks. They enjoyed just being together again. But there was no one for Cornelia to visit with. When she slipped into the kitchen, there was Mother, helping Aunt Gerda put the food onto the table. Two Russian girls were helping too.

"You've gone to too much work," said Mother.

"Ach, no. I still feel as if Agatha is my daughter. I am doing no more than I ought to do." Then she saw Cornelia standing uncertainly in the doorway. "It is full in here," she remarked. "Better go play."

Embarrassed, Cornelia backed out again. Bernhard had deserted her. He had disappeared into the Summer Room. There were thumping sounds coming from that corner of the house. Cornelia would have been interested to find out what was going on there. But it would be thought improper for her to investigate. So she turned to the little room where she and Anton and their parents were to sleep. The trundlebed was for Anton. You pulled it out from under the parents' bed, like a drawer. The hay-filled sack on the floor would be her mattress. Cornelia sat down on it and sighed.

Eating would be a long affair, a late affair. First the men would have their turn. Then the women and babies. Next the young people and last of all the children. At eleven you could never be sure where you belonged. The safest thing was to stay out of the way until someone called you. She wouldn't mind going to bed without supper—that is, she would *rather* do that than feel uncertain like this. But it would be considered unmannerly.

Even when Cornelia heard Martha's voice she did not stir. Martha was being very polite to Mother in an almost grownup way, asking about the trip. Finally she got round to asking for Cornelia.

"Where is she? Is she still such a little strip of a thing?"

Aunt Gerda laughed. "She's still a little strip. A dark strip. A whole Harms."

Well, why not? thought Cornelia resentfully. What was so good about being big and blond?

"Hey, you!" Martha bounced into the little room. "In the dark you sit here? Are you being *neksch*? (balky) Come out in the light where I can look at you."

The light in the kitchen made Cornelia blink at first. But then she studied Martha as steadily as Martha was studying her. A giggle came from Martha.

"My, you're small!"

"My, you're big!" Cornelia wasn't smiling at all.

"And so dark-skinned! Like one of those gypsies!"

SOME OF THE MENNONITE COLONIES
IN THE UKRAINE, RUSSIA

"And so pale-skinned!" Cornelia wagged her head pityingly. "You're not sick, are you?"

"Cornelia!" whispered Mother in amazement.

Aunt Gerda forced a laugh. "That's a *keck* (pert) child, that one. Martha, take her somewhere to play."

Just then, fortunately, Grandmother Siemens arrived. She lived across the way from her son Johann, and she was Mother's mother. She kissed Mother, patted Anton's spikey round head, and reached for Cornelia. "Ah, my dear little Cornelia! Still the same bright *Liebling* (darling)," she said, and she gave Cornelia a big hug. "What, Martha? You want to take her away with you? No, no. No, no. For five years my eyes have hungered for a sight of her. She stays with me tonight. We have much to discuss."

She took Cornelia into a corner of the Big Room. Suddenly it did not matter that there were other people crowding it. She and Grandmother chatted together like old friends. Martha joined them too, and that was all right. With Grandmother there to hear, she knew better than to twit Cornelia with being so dark and small.

Time slipped by happily. The men had gone to eat, Bernhard with them. Now it was the women's turn.

"Come, Mother. Come, Martha," said Aunt Gerda, poking her head through the doorway.

"What about Cornelia?" said Martha.

"Ach, she can eat with the children. She's too small to eat from the bowl, and we have *pluma moos* for supper."

"The two of us, Cornelia and I, will eat right here," said Grandmother pleasantly but decidedly. "Don't worry, Gerda. Martha, send one of the kitchen girls with some food. We can use the little table—or a chair, maybe. And be sure to tell her I like my coffee *hot*."

34

The food came. *Pluma moos*, thick slices of boiled ham, small buns, the kind that were always served at engagement parties. Coffee for Grandmother, a cup of milk for Cornelia. She could tell by the appearance and smell that everything was very tasty. Aunt Gerda was a very good cook. Everybody said so. But Cornelia could only nibble tonight. There was a large knot in her throat. Food could not crowd past it.

Her eyes felt hot and dry. Why did Aunt Gerda always try so hard to say hurtful things? If Martha said something about Cornelia's size and color no one minded. But if *she* said the same sort of thing about Martha, she was the *keck* one.

"Here, child," said Grandmother. "Why are you so sober? Do you know something? Aunt Gerda is taking your mother and Agatha to Steinbach tomorrow. There is much work to be done before the wedding. They will be making plans, and visiting some of Wilhelm's relatives. They will leave early. And I am going to ask if you can come and stay with me. Will you like that?"

Cornelia cheered up instantly. Grandmother Siemens was a good story teller, almost as good as Father. The thing was settled before Cornelia crawled under the featherbed on her haysack mattress for the night. She would have been happier if Martha were going to go to Steinbach too. Aunt Gerda wanted to take her, but for once Martha chose to stay with Cornelia and their grandmother.

Long before the children were out of bed next morning the carriage had left for Steinbach. The younger children ate breakfast with only the Russian girls to serve them. Martha always was nicer when there were no grownups to praise her. She even fooled around a bit with Johann and Anton while they were eating their cracklings and brown bread, and drinking milk. Then the boys ran out to play, and the girls skipped across the road to Grandmother Siemens' little house.

Compared to Martha's home this seemed almost like a playhouse, but it was stuffed full of interesting things. There was a Grandmother smell about the place, mixed today with peppermint. Grandmother was baking pepper-nuts, and the girls were allowed to help her arrange the little lumps of dough on the bun pans.

Cornelia never forgot this day. Grandmother began telling stories of the early years after the Mennonites came to settle in Russia. The first ones came 85 years ago, in 1789. That was before Grandmother was born. They came in long, slow trains, hundreds and hundreds of them in one train. *Human* trains. They *walked*. They walked over 1200 miles. Only those who were feeble with age, or too young to walk, rode—on wheelbarrows. All their household belongings were loaded onto two-wheel carts, drawn by people in turn. At night they camped along the roadside, and moved on again, day after day after day.

Most of the countryside was empty of people. Miles and miles of wilderness! Where they met Russian peasants they were kindly received. But you had to be wary of them too. They were as ready to cheat and rob their guests as they had been to welcome them.

"But—where did all the Mennonites come from?" said Cornelia, puzzled.

"From Prussia. And before that, from Holland."

"But why? Why are they always moving and moving along?"

"Because of broken promises," said Grandmother

solemnly. "Look, children. We Mennonites follow the teachings of Menno Simons. We follow the ways of peace. We do not want our sons to grow up to fight and kill people. In Holland our people were persecuted because of their faith. So they moved to Prussia, because the nobility promised them freedom from going to war. They were given poor land. That did not matter, if only they could live in peace. They worked hard and soon they improved the land, so they made a good living. Then the Prussian neighbors said, 'Look at these Mennonites. They won't fight—yet see what good land they have!' So the law was changed. It said that Mennonites had to fight like everyone else. But just about then, Catherine the Great of Russia said, 'Come to my country. I will be your mother. I will give you land. I need good farmers who are willing to work hard. Come to me. Here in Russia you will never need to fight. You can work in peace, for everlasting times.' So we came."

"And now the Czar has broken the promise," said Cornelia, nibbling a bit of peppermint dough. It stung her tongue.

"Who said?" said Martha, looking alarmed.

"Father. All of Schoenthal. In the Bergthal colony *everybody* is talking about it."

Grandmother sighed. "I'm afraid it is true. Czar Alexander has said that he can no longer allow us Mennonites to be treated differently from all the other people. What is to become of us I do not know."

"Maybe *we* are moving, too," said Cornelia. For a moment she enjoyed the shock her words brought. "To Canada. Maybe."

Martha looked blank. "Canada?" Where's that?"

"On the other side of the world," said Cornelia

37

breezily. "You have to cross a big ocean to get there."

"Well, but— How can anybody go to the other side of the world?"

Maybe, thought Cornelia, maybe Martha believed too that the world is flat! Grandmother wasn't worrying about the shape of the earth. She had sunk into a chair beside the table. "Moving! My Sarah! So far away!"

Cornelia felt sorry instantly. "Maybe not, Grandmother. Maybe not." She hugged her grandmother.

"Has Peter— Has your father talked about it?"

"Only once. He promised not to go if Mother doesn't want to. Grandmother, tell about the winter of the big snowstorm."

"That was in 1847," began Grandmother obediently. Her voice, absent-minded at first, grew stronger as she went along. "The storm began at Christmas time, on the second holiday (Dec. 26). A strong wind arose, and it blew in the snow. The earth had been dry and powdery, so the first snow was almost black. But the wind kept blowing, and the clouds kept on emptying their load. For three weeks the storm raged. All the houses got darker and darker, as snow piled up against the windows. It covered the roofs next. A house like this one would have been buried completely, chimney and all."

"That winter we learned how wise our forefathers were to build the house and barn together. Nobody could have gone outdoors to take care of the horses and cows. But the roofs almost broke from the weight of the snow. And some people and animals almost starved."

The girls shivered pleasurably. "Tell about the big hailstorm," they begged next. "Tell about the earthquake . . . ." "Tell about the winter when so many sheep died . . ." For hours they kept Grandmother busy

38

remembering. The peppernuts had come out of the oven, brown and fragrant. The girls munched handfuls while they listened to stories.

Cornelia knew all of them. She had heard Father and Mother tell them often. But still she begged for more and more. "Tell about the gophers."

Grandmother laughed. "Your mother, Cornelia, was nine then, and your father, Martha, was 11. You must know, children, that the crops looked good that year, very good. But that spring was the spring of the *susliki* (gophers). Thousands and thousands of *susliki*. So what did the *Schulzenbott* decide? Every family must bring 80 dead gophers to the *Schulze*. Your Grandfather, the sailor, was on the Black Sea, on a sailing vessel. So I and the children, we went out to hunt *susliki*."

"How?"

"Oh, the holes were everywhere, everywhere. And there was enough water in the ponds. We drowned the troublesome animals. We poured water down the holes. We stood waiting with heavy sticks. When they popped up, down came the stick. So! Another gopher for the *Schulze*! With God's help we saved the crop."

"But it wasn't your crop."

"No, we were of the landless ones. Your grandfather Siemens was the second son of a wealthy man. His older brother got the farm and the machinery and animals."

"But—but that's not fair!"

"That is the law. That was the way Catherine the Great wanted it. The estates must not be broken up. So your grandfather became a sailor."

"It's not fair! It's not fair!" sputtered Cornelia.

"It's the law," said Grandmother again.

Cornelia thought of something else. "But Uncle Johann. *He* has land. Why is that?"

"Oh-ho!" Grandmother laughed till her apron front shook. "Your Uncle Johann married an heiress. Aunt Gerda—your mother, Martha—was the oldest daugher of a man who had land but no sons."

That's why she is so bossy, thought Cornelia. The land, the house, *everything* belongs to *her*!

The girls were tired of sitting still, so Grandmother opened her chest. She showed them things their sailor grandfather brought from many strange places. There were fancy scarves, tablecloths, a beautiful fan, a tiny oil lamp that looked like a cream pitcher. The girls had fun running their fingers over the smooth satins and silks. From the bottom of the chest Grandmother pulled out a battered rag doll.

"Do you remember this, Cornelia? You used to play with it all day long."

Cornelia sat on the floor, looking earnestly at the doll that had lost one shoe-button eye, and whose rusty wool hair was tangled and unkempt looking. Something stirred in her, as though she could almost remember. Almost.

Grandmother and Martha were busy repacking all the pretty things. At last Cornelia laid the doll gently on top of a brilliant satin brocade headscarf, and patted it down. So the heavy lid of the chest would not crush its face too badly.

After dinner Grandmother said, "Run out and see if any of my cherries are ripe. Or go and swing on the hundred year oak. I need a nap."

"May we eat some cherries?"

"All you want. But go, go. I'm not as young as I used to be." She gave each a push, smiling.

So the cousins ran out to the orchard. One of

Grandmother's trees was famous all through the Molotschna settlement, said Martha. Its cherries ripened so early, and their flavor was so superior. Most of the fruit was a pale red still, too green to pick. But here and there were round jewels of clear scarlet. For about five minutes the girls picked busily and happily, eating a few, but dropping most of them into the pouches formed when they held up their aprons. With lapfuls of cherries they went to sit in the sun beside Grandmother's woodshed.

"Know something?" asked Martha after a while, sounding suddenly moody. "Grandmother loves you better than me."

Cornelia said nothing. She felt guilty, because she had just been thinking the very same thing.

"And it's silly. It's not fair at all. Because she isn't really your grandmother as much as she is mine."

"She is too!" Cornelia's eyes flashed. "Do you think that just because I live so far away—"

Martha laughed. "Your really think she is your very own Grandmother? Huh!"

Cornelia popped a cherry into her mouth. She chewed, spit out the stone.

"What do you mean—*Huh*?"

"I mean, *Huh*! I mean you probably don't even know that Aunt Sarah isn't your real mother."

If the ground and grass on which she was sitting had suddenly slid out from under her— If the sun had swooped across the sky and out of sight— If, in that instant, Cornelia had found herself alone in the howling wilderness of a snowstorm, she could hardly have been more jolted than she was. Mother—her *step*mother? That must be what Martha meant. But, it *couldn't* be. Why, her memory went back, ever so far. Ever so. And always

41

there was Mother, and Grandmother, and Bernhard—Cornelia jumped up. The remainder of her cherries rolled into the tall grasses.

"Hey, you dropped them!"

"I'm full. Let's go to the hundred-year oak."

But Martha was scrambling around on her knees, picking up the twinkling red balls.

Cornelia thought, It mustn't be! It mustn't be true! But a dull heavy voice whispered, but it is. It's true.

She remembered things. She remembered people saying, "The older three certainly have the Fehdrau look." She used to think that was funny when she wasn't a Fehdrau at all! Once she said to Bernhard, "I'm glad we don't have a stepmother, aren't you?" And he just smiled his affectionate smile, and he said, "You're a funny girl." But nobody, nobody ever told her. Maybe they thought she knew.

Martha, still on her knees, said, "Why are you so quiet? How could I know that you didn't know about Aunt Sarah? You're such a funny girl. For eleven years you're so little—and you *know* so little."

Cornelia might have retorted, "*Who* knows so little? *You* probably think the earth is flat!" But she didn't. She felt numb all over. There was a stone, cold and hard and heavy, in her chest somewhere. It wouldn't allow her to talk.

They ran out to the oak tree in the middle of the village. Cornelia in the lead, Martha pounding and panting behind her, "Don't go so fast, Nelia. Don't go so fast!"

There was a rope swing, and some girls were using it by turns. Cornelia began climbing the tree. It had wide spreading branches, just right for climbing. But a gasp

42

went up from all the little girls when Cornelia went skimming up.

"Oooooh! Girls don't climb trees!"

Well, I do, thought Cornelia. She found a crotch that was just right for a seat, and the leaves closed her in, nice and private.

"Who's she?" she heard the girls say.

"My cousin. From the Bergthal colony."

"That's far," said someone, sounding impressed. Maybe they thought that if you travelled so far, no wonder you were different. Wild like.

"And her sister Agatha is going to marry Wilhelm Franz," volunteered Martha.

There were excited squeals and murmurs. Everyone knew about the big Franz estate.

The girls kept swinging, but Cornelia's private place hardly stirred. Some girls ran away after a while. New ones kept coming. When they tired of swinging they played Drop the Handkerchief. And still Cornelia sat thinking. Stepmother. Mother is my *stepmother*. The stone inside her kept growing. By now it crowded her breathing.

"Cornelia?" Martha's voice drifted up timidly. "It's almost supper time, and I have to go or Mother will scold. Aren't you coming down?"

Cornelia shook herself. It was like coming out of a long sleep. There was nobody under the big tree but Martha, yet Cornelia hadn't noticed the others leaving.

She let herself fall from branch to branch, then she slipped down the trunk the rest of the way.

"You've torn your apron!" said Martha, shocked. "What ever will Aunt Sarah say?"

She will say, Why didn't you take better care? thought

Cornelia as she trotted silently homeward with Martha. She will not lecture me.

"Aren't you—aren't you *ever* going to talk to me again?"

For a moment Cornelia forgot the stone inside her. Martha! She was practically *begging* to be friends. This had never happened before.

Of course, Aunt Gerda noticed the hole in the apron instantly. The women had returned from their visit to Steinbach. They were in the kitchen looking at pieces of cloth, and discussing how they should be made up into dresses. As usual, Aunt Gerda thought her own ideas were much the best, and it seemed to Cornelia that mostly Agatha agreed with her rather than with Mother.

"Well, you are the one who will be wearing the dresses," said Mother, giving in.

That was when Cornelia and Martha entered the room. So, there in plain sight, was the tear—and there, too, was Cornelia's hair, all tangled as usual.

"Look at the two girls. Been together all day. Look at the difference," said Aunt Gerda good-humoredly.

Cornelia didn't have to look. She knew Martha's hair would be smooth and shiny. It always was. Cornelia's head bobbed as Mother undid the tight braids and combed the hair and rebraided it.

"Put on a clean apron," she whispered. "Go."

But of course, it really was too late. Aunt Gerda could make a hole in her niece's apron last half through suppertime. She had seen what she had seen, and she kept on about "my Martha" and how neat and clever she was.

Tonight the children ate at a separate table in the middle room. The boys were noisy, laughing and talking about the fun they had had that day. Through the noise

Cornelia, who sat near the connecting door, could hear Aunt Gerda's voice, loud and positive.

"What I've said before, I say again, Peter. If you want to be so foolish as to go so far away, you should leave your family here. At least your girls. Agatha is well taken care of. I have seen to that. Cornelia could learn much from my Martha."

Cornelia's heart was doing strange things. But her father remained silent.

Then Mother spoke up. "How could we even *dream* of leaving our little daughter behind?"

Almost before Cornelia knew what she was going to do she had slipped through the Big Room, through the entry, and was out in the passage, groping in the dark. The stone in her chest was crowding her throat. She had to be alone. She had to be alone. She felt all over the lefthand wall. No doorknob. Then she tried the righthand wall. A moment later her trembling legs were taking her up a dark stairway to the storage space.

It was a daunting thing, going into an unknown storeroom without a light after dark. But Cornelia's need to be private was greater than her fears of shadows and mice. She recognized the dry dusty smell of a heap of grain before her toes touched the edge of the heap. The next moment she had crumpled, and was burying her face in it. The hurt in her chest gave way. It was like the bursting of a dam, like the breakup of ice on the river in spring.

She thought, bewildered, Why am I crying? Mother called me "our daughter." She said they would never leave me behind. So why am I crying?— But she kept right on, harder than ever.

Finally she grew quiet. After a while she heard people

calling her name. She heard Aunt Gerda exclaiming, "Where has that child disappeared to?" Then through her swollen eyelids she saw a faint flicker of light climbing the rafters. Someone was feeling her way up the stairs. It was Mother. She was alone.

Afterwards, long afterwards, Cornelia remembered this day. Grandmother's cherry tree was always mixed up in the memory, along with the hundred-year oak, and a huge upstairs storeroom, with a candle flickering dimly, and Mother sitting on the damp wheat beside her.

"We thought you *knew*" said Mother, when Cornelia had admitted what had been troubling her. "I'm sure we never thought that you didn't know. I certainly never tried to make you believe that I was your very own mother."

And on the day which began with Grandmother's stories about old times, Cornelia heard things about her own childhood that she had, somehow, never known before.

Her mother—Agatha Fehdrau Harms—died a few days after Cornelia was born.

"It was very sad, a sad time for me. My dearest friend gone, and so suddenly. But it was sadder for your father. Perhaps this is why we have not talked about it much. You were so tiny and frail, nobody expected you to live. They postponed your mother's funeral for a few days, thinking they might bury the baby with its mother." Mother's voice held a trembling laugh now. "But there was a spunky spark in the dark-eyed mite even then. Aunt Gerda had a baby of her own, besides a houseful of other children. She offered to take Agatha. But no one knew quite what to do with the sickly two-year-old, Bernhard, and with you. Your mother had worried so

46

much about you both at the last. When she asked me if I would care for you as long as you lived, what could I say but yes? So— I took you."

"Since I was living with Grandmother still, she had a say-so too, of course. But she was glad to have two babies to take care of."

"So that was why," murmured Cornelia. "When Martha told me today—that—that you weren't really my m-mother at all— I tried to remember. I tried so hard, my head aches. But I couldn't remember any time when you and Grandmother weren't there."

"Yes, that's why. We took care of you every day, and every day we came to love you more. On weekends your father would stay out at Uncle Johann's and Aunt Gerda's and we would bring you and Bernhard there, so all of you could be together. Secretly I used to worry. What if your father should remarry! What if he'd take you away from me? Well, one day he told me he was thinking of getting married again, and since I was mothering his children, would I consider becoming his wife, too? So—we were married."

And Mother, who rarely kissed any of her children, stooped to kiss Cornelia, and they shared a long, silent hug. "Come," she said matter-of-factly then. "We'd better go down."

Cornelia held back. "What will Aunt Gerda say?" she whispered in panic.

Mother whispered back, "Come. We'll slip out through the barn, where it's dark, and we'll run across to Grandmother's place."

Father was there ahead of them, having come to look for Cornelia. Grandmother helped rinse her face with cold water. Then they sat down and visited. It was nice here, nice and peaceful.

47

The following week Aunt Gerda took Agatha and her mother, and Martha, to the nearest city, Melitopol, for a shopping excursion. They would be gone several days and nights. Martha offered to stay with her cousin, but Cornelia really preferred to stay at home without her. Grandmother was there, right across the way. And Father, who meant to look up old friends, said Bernhard and Cornelia might as well take the opportunity to get better acquainted with their birthplace.

That was an interesting week. Father took them from place to place, to mills and factories, to smithies and shoemaker shops. He used to be a mill hand before he left for Prussia to study to become a teacher. Some said that he had become proud and big headed. But they soon forgot their grumpiness. Cornelia discovered that her father could be very funny. There was much laughter wherever they went.

You could not help noticing that these people did not think about migrating nearly as strongly as the Bergthalers did. There was talk about the twelve "spies"— and a lot of wondering about what they were seeing and experiencing in the land of bears and wild Indians! And about what their reports would be. But most of the people seemed to have made up their minds to stay where they were.

"Why is that, Father?" said Bernhard when they were out on the road again.

"There are several reasons. Molotschna is a much richer colony than Bergthal. The soil is more productive. There are fewer landless families, and better job opportunities for those who are landless. And because the people are more comfortable it would cost more for them to leave all behind and seek new homes."

"It hasn't anything to do with the war question, has it, Father?" remarked Bernhard.

"So it would seem."

Cornelia asked a question that had been troubling her. "Do the people here look down on the Bergthalers?"

"I'm afraid so."

"But that's not right!"

"It's not right," agreed her father. "But it's human nature."

"Why? Why would they?"

So Father explained. The Bergthalers were considered narrow. They were more stern, more severe, more closed. *They* thought the Molotschna people were too worldly. In school, for instance, a Bergthal teacher was allowed to use no textbooks except the Bible, the *Fibel* (primer), a grammar, and an arithmetic book. And a map or two. Much learning was considered dangerous. At 14 a child had learned enough. But here in the Molotschna colony a few young men were going away to study in Prussian and Russian universities.

Cornelia and Bernhard exchanged a smile when their father mentioned the books. It was an old family joke. Father wasn't allowed to use the other books in school. But he read them at home, and in school he told "stories." That was safe. That was all right. Cornelia was half envious of the Molotschna children, though. Imagine being able to go to a school where you could use books and more books!

"Well, here's the old Fehdrau mill," announced Father. He smiled. "This is where I first met your mother. I was seventeen—and I thought her very, very beautiful."

A cousin of Aunt Gerda's owned the mill now. Ernst Fehdrau was a stocky man with a white bristly beard. He was friendly, in a serious kind of way. He called Peter Harms "brother Harms."

"If you children want to have a look around, go," he said, with a wave of his arm. "I'm sure you'll be *gescheit* (sensible) enough to keep out of mischief and danger." Then he and Father perched on sacks of grain, and began a long earnest conversation.

Cornelia and her brother poked around a bit, but managed to keep within earshot most of the time.

Ever since moving to Schoenthal, Peter Harms had been teaching a weekly Bible class in the home. Some of the *Ohms* (preachers) were opposed to it, he told Mr. Fehdrau. Two came occasionally. And the *Oberschulze* came all the time. So the class was not stopped. It puzzled Cornelia why anyone would want to stop the classes. They were studying the *Bible*. What could possibly be wrong with that?

"Don't misunderstand me," Cornelia heard her father say earnestly. "They are sincere people, and the gospel of Jesus Christ is all there in the sermons they read and listen to on Sundays. But the people are unschooled, they speak the Low German in their homes. The sermons, which are taken from books, are deep and difficult to understand. If you ask the average church member he'll tell you that one cannot know that his sins are pardoned. The best they know of is to hope—and to keep on hoping."

"Poor people. Poor, poor people," murmured the miller. "But you, Brother Harms— If the Bergthal move to the new world—"

"As I am almost certain they will," interjected Peter Harms.

"Then what about you?"

Father was silent for a while. "You know why I moved to the Bergthal colony in the first place. I could have had a better teaching position here—But I felt, and my Sarah agreed with me, that God had work for me there. I am willing to cross the ocean, if God calls."

"And your Sarah?"

Peter Harms hesitated. "God can make her heartily willing too. Come, children. It is time we go, I think."

And it was. The carriage from Melitopol was home before them. And for the next days there was little time to think about anything but getting ready for the wedding. Aunt Gerda insisted that everybody from Father to Anton had to have new clothes. Cornelia couldn't see why. Everybody would naturally be wearing black clothes for the wedding. They *had* black clothes. What difference did it make if they were not new? But Aunt Gerda said they must not be put to shame before the Franz relations. And since she was paying for the cloth, and had hired two seamstresses to do the sewing, she had her way.

Black clothes for church, summery ones for later. All the relations would be going to the Gerhard Franz estate for dinner and supper.

Father's part in the preparations was the prettiest of all, thought Cornelia. He wrote the invitation letter. He could write beautifully.

"For the wedding of our daughter Agatha, to the *Juengling* (young man), Wilhelm Franz, which, if the Lord wills, is to take place in the Steinfeld Mennonite church on Sunday, May 13, 1873, we invite you, so that together we may pray down the blessings of God on the young pair." That's what he wrote on one side of the sheet of paper. On the other side there was a list of names of those who were especially invited. Each one who got the letter was expected to carry it to the name that was next on the list.

Cornelia's black dress was fancier than any she had ever worn before. It was trimmed with ruffles and lace. The sleeves and skirt were stiffly lined, and she felt hot but very important as she sat between her mother and sister in the large church.

It was built exactly like the Bergthaler church, even if it was so much larger. The platform was narrow and long, and it ran along the center section of one side wall. The row of chairs on the platform was meant for all the *Ohms* and the *Vorsaenger* (song leaders). The door into the church was in the centre of the opposite wall. All the women and girls sat to the left of the aisle, the men and boys to the right. Wilhelm, in his new black suit, sat between his father and Uncle Johann Siemens. The church was crowded today because of the wedding.

At ten o'clock the *Ohms* came in, all six of them. They moved solemnly up the aisle. Halfway they stopped. "The peace of God be with us all! Amen!" called out one of the *Ohms*. It had a very holy sound, thought Cornelia. Then they walked on again—up the steps and to the waiting chairs.

It was a long service. There were three preachers who spoke—and nobody said a word about a wedding! There was singing at the beginning, and again later. Twice everyone knelt for silent prayer. Finally, finally, the chief *Ohm* stood up to make an announcement. "There are two persons here," he said, as if he just happened to remember, "who have asked to be united in marriage. Wilhelm Franz and Agatha Harms, would you come forward please?"

It seemed strange to see Agatha walking forward alone like that. Brave. But her voice shook and so did Wilhelm's when they answered the *Ohm's* questions.

Afterwards there was laughter and teasing and feasting. All the wedding guests drove or rode or walked to the Franz estate. Aunt Gerda had wanted to serve the noon meal at her house, but Mrs. Franz said no. Since Agatha's parents could not provide the meal, being so far from their home, it was only proper and right that Wilhelm's parents should do so.

All the girls were glad to get out of their stiff black dresses and into light summer clothes. The weather was fine, and tables had been placed under the orchard trees. House-servants flitted about, serving the guests. And afterwards all the young people played circle games on the grassy yard while the older people sat watching and visiting.

The Gerhard Franzes had seventy yard servants! Grinning, they came with a chair, and Wilhelm, their young master, had to sit in it. Laughing and cheering, they carried him all around the yard.

After it was all over, the Franz carriage took the Harmses back to Schoenthal again. They left Agatha behind. Cornelia hadn't thought it would hurt so much.

III
For Bernhard's Sake

The hill north of Schoenthal was long, and level on top. Almost as level as a wall. But it had a lovely slope, covered with grass and dotted with brush. Whenever the weather was fine, the slope was a favorite playground for Schoenthal children. The view from the top was lovely. The village and the whole valley lay before you—the winding little river, and the long and narrow fields that gave the valley a stripy look. No wonder, thought Cornelia, that they had given the village its name— Beautiful Valley. It was like a song in your heart and an ache in your throat. It was odd. How could a thing that was so lovely be both sad and glad?

Today the wind came skipping over the top of the hill. Cornelia, climbing the slope with her brothers, laughed in the face of the wind. "I'll race you to the top!" she called.

There was an instant scramble, as Johann and Anton tried to outclimb her. They couldn't do it! She was using the brush to help her along. Her arms pulling and her legs pushing, she outdistanced them easily. Now she was at the top, and the wind billowed her long skirts around. Cornelia laughed in triumph. There came Johann and Anton. Their faces were crimson, their lips set. But where was Bernhard?

She looked anxiously down the way she had come. There were children, dozens of children, at play all over. They were capering in the wind, or playing Tag or Leapfrog. But she could not see Bernhard anywhere.

On the instant the sense of fun and triumph drained out of Cornelia. She was frightened. How could she have forgotten? In Molotschna Father took Bernhard to see a doctor. Both of them looked grave when they came back, and Father warned Cornelia that her brother must never tire himself again. Never again.

Scrambling, stumbling, slithering, and scrambling on again, Cornelia went down the slope as fast as she dared. Anxiously her eyes scanned the slope. *Bernhard.* Where could he be?

As far back as she could remember, her older brother had never been strong in body. She was as thin as he, but she was full of bounce and fire and activity. Always. Bernhard was slow moving and gentle. And he had those horrid coughing spells. Whenever he laughed a lot or hurried too much, the ugly spells came, almost choking him. Then everyone grew anxious, and he would be blue and weak for hours.

In her mad scramble Cornelia came to the little spring that bubbled out of the hillside. Bernhard lay on his side beside the water. His narrow shoulders were heaving.

"Are you feeling bad, Bernhard? Are you feeling bad?" stammered Cornelia anxiously.

He moved his head so he could see her. There was blood on his chin, and a spot of red in the grass. He was smiling, but his lips were blue and he did not try to talk. She knelt quickly, cupping her hands to fill them with water. She brought the living cup to his lips. He drank a bit. Cornelia dipped her apron hem into the stream and wiped his face. He was shivering, so she sat on the windy side of him to shield him. For a long while neither of them moved or said a word.

From where she sat, Cornelia could see farmers moving

up and down their narrow strips of ripened grain. They swayed rhythmically as they cut the grain with scythes. Women and girls followed behind. Using handfuls of straw, they tied the cut grain into bundles. So much activity—and here lay Bernhard, weak and helpless. Cornelia felt sadder by the minute.

Gradually Bernhard's breathing became easier. They could think of going home slowly now.

As soon as their mother saw their faces she guessed what had happened. She made Bernhard drink some milk and then go to bed. He said he wasn't hungry. After he had disappeared into the boys' room Cornelia looked at her mother with wide frightened eyes.

"Was it bad?" whispered Mother.

"The worst I have ever seen. And it was my fault. I made him hurry too much. I forgot. Oh, how could I forget?"

"Shshsh . . . . Don't blame yourself too much. He forgot, too. There come the boys. Run to open the door, Cornelia. Tell them to come in quietly."

It was a strange evening. Everyone spoke in whispers. They walked on tiptoe. There was no door-slamming. Every half hour Mother checked to see if Bernhard was still sleeping. How they all wished that Father were at home! But he had left eight days ago for Chortitza colony to attend a conference with the *Oberschulze*.

The deputies had come back from America, and there was a big general meeting of interested Mennonites in Russia to hear their report. All Bergthal colony was buzzing with talk about the migration. Soon now they would know if Schoenthal would be migrating. And if the village went, what about the Peter Harms family? That was a question only Sarah Harms could decide.

56

She had made up a bed for Johann and Anton in the Middle Room this evening so Bernhard need not be disturbed. Cornelia had gone to sit on the stone porch in front of the teacherage. The wind had died down. The sun was setting. The whole village was settling down for night. It was beautiful and peaceful. But sad, too, somehow.

After a time Mother came to sit beside her. For a while they just sat, not exchanging a word. And every minute, it seemed, Cornelia's heart was getting heavier.

"We must not give up hope," said Mother at last, as if she had been able to read Cornelia's thoughts.
"But—but—what's *wrong* with him?"
"Bernhard has what your father and I have long suspected— He has *Schwindsucht*." (consumption, tuberculosis)

Like Lena Schultz's first mother, thought Cornelia numbly. Like Johannes Pauls. Like Menno Funk. They got thinner and thinner. Day by day they grew weaker. And finally they died.

"The doctor at Melitopol told your father that a sea voyage might help him a great deal."
"Then we're going, aren't we?"

Mother sighed. "One needs money for the trip. We have no money. And what would we do after we arrived in the new country? Your father has never built anything. Not even a woodbox. He is a gifted man *in his line*. But you know how he is at swinging a hammer! How could he build a house for us?"

"He could teach the children—and their fathers could build the house!"

Teaching was an important work—and Cornelia knew her father was a good teacher.

Mother said, "Cornelia, don't think that I do not care. About Bernhard. About the migration. About your father's desire to go to the new country. He is wise in many ways. He believes that bad times are coming for Russia. For hundreds of years the poor people have been treated very much like slaves. Your father believes—and so do many thoughtful men of our people—that there's going to be a revolution in this land."

Revolution! Cornelia shivered. Father had told her about the one in France a hundred years ago. "Will it be as bad as that one?"

"Worse. Much worse. That is what your father says. But, Cornelia, we don't *know* that it's coming. What I do know is that your father is not capable of building a house for his family, or of farming land that has never been ploughed before. He knows very little about cattle, and I know even less. I did not grow up on a farm, you know. And I have to be *practical* about this matter."

"But—Bernhard," said Cornelia.

"Yes. There's Bernhard." Mother sat with her hands clasped around her knees, the toes of her shoes just peeking out from under her skirts. She gazed before her broodingly. "He was so little, so frail, when I promised your mother that I would take care of him. Often he was near death, because it seemed he had to catch every child's disease that went through the village. He looked most of the time as if a slight puff of wind would blow out the flicker of life. But—he continued to live. God must have heard our prayers. We certainly prayed. Cornelia, he could not be dearer to me if he really were my own boy. Can you believe that?"

"Yes. He's so good."

Unexpectedly Mother laughed. She gave Cornelia a light spank. "I love my spunky daughter, too. Just as much. Now run along to bed. It's high time."

When Cornelia awoke next morning the first thing she heard was Father's voice as he joked with Anton and Johann. He had come home during the night.

That evening there was a *Schulzenbott*—a gathering of all the fathers of the village. This time it did not matter whether they owned land or not. The *Oberschulze* said this concerned all households alike. He and Teacher Harms were going to report on the conference at Chortitza. Village by village the Bergthal colony must decide if it wanted to seek a new home in the new world or not.

The day had been hot, and the evening was sultry. All the windows of the schoolroom were open wide, and so was the door. It ought to be easy to hear some of the discussion by sitting out on the porch, thought Cornelia. But that plan was spoiled. Several women came with their husbands. Not to attend the meeting of course. That would never do. They visited the teacher's wife in the kitchen and they talked so loudly it was impossible to hear anything else.

Cornelia ran around the house to the other side. Yes, the windows on that side were open, too. And Bernhard was there ahead of her, sitting in the grass, leaning against the schoolhouse. Cornelia sank down beside him.

They could hear just about everything. But part of the discussion made Cornelia impatient. Why was it that grownups always had to have things *repeated* in such detail—things that everybody knew already? Everyone in Schoenthal knew why they were thinking of migrating.

Everyone knew that the Czar had broken the promise his grandmother made to the Mennonites. That he said now that Mennonite young men would have to go into the army, just like everyone else. That he had agreed they could do medical work instead of actually fighting, if they prefered. But they would have to wear the regular uniform, and live in barracks, along with the soldiers, just as if they were of them.

The *Oberschulze* reported that he and Teacher Harms had just returned from the conference in Chortitza— (Everyone knew *that* too!)

"I can't see what good it did for Peter Harms to go," interrupted a strong, hoarse voice. Solomon Schultz's! He was Lena Schultz's father. "It is hardly possible that the landless ones among us will be able to bear the expenses of the trip."

A clamour of voices broke out, many people talking at once. Then the *Oberschulze* shushed the noise, and only his voice could be heard.

"If we are honest—if this migration is a matter of conscience with us, as we profess that it is—then everyone must be allowed to go. Everyone. Every man, woman, and child who wants to. No one among us is too poor. The rich will help pay the expenses of the poor."

"What about their debts?" someone called out.

"*We* don't have any debts!" whispered Cornelia indignantly.

"Shhhh!" said Bernhard.

"The debts, too, will be paid—by all of us—all who can help, according to our means. When we move—if we move—we will go with a clean slate. Is that under-stood?" He sounded almost fierce. But Jakob Penner wasn't really a fierce man, and everyone knew that.

"Now I am asking Teacher Harms to report on the conference, and especially on the report brought back by the twelve deputies who travelled to North America."

Father spoke more quietly than the others. Cornelia and Bernhard had to strain their ears to hear. He told about the land the men had seen in Manitoba, Canada, and in the Dakotas, in Kansas, and in Nebraska of the United States. He said that the Bergthaler deputies, Peters and Wiebe, were most impressed with the opportunities offered in Canada. For one thing, the Canadian government was so anxious for settlers that it had offered to pay half the travel expenses of every individual. This amounted to thirty dollars for each person over eight years of age, fifteen for those between a year and eight years of age, and three dollars for the babies. The deputies said that the opportunity for settlement in Canada were limitless.

"Is it not true—" broke in Solomon Schultz. He always had to side against everyone else. "Is it not true that most of the deputies found Manitoba very discouraging? I have been told that there are many Indians. At one place the men were almost killed by Indians—and they were rescued by soldiers from the fort at Winnipeg. Is that not so?"

"They were Metis, not Indians, for one thing," corrected Peter Harms. "And the whole incident was due to an unfortunate misunderstanding. It is also true that the deputies were welcomed into some Indian homes and shown every hospitality. And everywhere they went, people slept with their windows unbarred at night. That is how much they feared the 'savage Indians'."

Some of the men laughed, but Solomon Schultz was not through.

"But is it not true that Ewert has said that the land in Manitoba is too wet, and that there are many grasshoppers and mosquitoes? Also, the winters are said to be long and hard, and very cold."

"It is true that the winters are cold," Father's patient voice went on. "But the land is good. One Indian farmer said that he planted two bushels of potatoes and harvested almost a hundred. And the land is free—160 acres to every male, eighteen years of age or older. Besides that, those who can afford it can purchase another 480 acres for a very modest price. Wet? It is well watered, the tract that has been offered to us. Three rivers drain the area. Besides these blessings, we could still live in colonies, separate from the other inhabitants. Our village life could go on just as we are accustomed to it. The schools would still be under our control. And we would be living under a monarch."

There was a murmur of many voices here. Most of the men seemed to feel that kings and queens were safer than a republic.

"What is your thinking?" said the *Oberschulze*. "Now that you have heard the report, are you in favor of migrating?"

Now, thought Cornelia, quivering with excitement. Now she'd soon know what she wanted so much to know.

That moment her mother stepped around the corner of the schoolhouse. "so this is where you sit!" she exclaimed in a whisper. "Bernhard, a storm is coming. You must not be out in it. Come, children."

Cornelia had not noticed that a wind had risen. Dark masses of cloud were climbing the sky rapidly, blotting out the early stars. Indoors, Cornelia helped to close the shutters of the windows. It made the house seem very stuffy. The women visitors still were chatting in the kitchen.

"Better go to bed, too" advised Mother.

Bernhard had gone without a protest. But Cornelia begged to sit up for Father. How could anyone go to bed without knowing the results of the vote? As usual, when there was a serious question to be settled each man would step singly up to the *Oberschulze* and give his vote by word of mouth.

Yes—or no? Was Schoenthal in favor of moving to North America? If so, would it choose Canada? If so, would the Peter Harms family go too? They might. The land was free there. Then the Harms family would never be landless again!

To go to a far country— From the start, the thought had excited Cornelia. But since yesterday she had a stronger reason for wanting to go. Bernhard must have his chance to get well. The doctor had said that a sea voyage sometimes did wonders for people with consumption.

Tonight Bernhard had not seemed much different than usual. A bit paler, maybe, and a bit weaker. He was jolly at suppertime, and joked with Father. But he seemed to be glad to go to bed just now. As for Cornelia, a great stone of anxiety rested on her heart. And the night matched her mood. It was black and restless, with a grumble of thunder in its throat.

The husbands of the visitors came to take their wives home. They left in a hurry to avoid the coming storm. For a while then there was a continuous flicker and rattle and roll. Then the rain came. It gushed down. And still Father had not returned from the meeting.

Cornelia had wedged herself into the corner behind the

table. Her legs were stretched out along the bench. She meant to keep awake until her father came home. But just in case she should fall asleep, she couldn't tumble off the bench this way.

It was a wet, wet night. Mother stood in the open doorway, leaning her head against the doorframe. What was she thinking about? About Bernhard? About going to Canada? Canada. Cornelia said the word over to herself. It would seem strange to live in a country by that name. *If* the Harmses moved.

"Sarah! Why are you standing in the open doorway like this?" Father exclaimed suddenly. "You're getting wet from the spray."

"Not nearly as wet as you are. You're soaked. To the skin."

He took off his shoes and set them on old cloths in the corner. In his stocking feet he squished around, talking excitedly. The vote was unanimous. Everyone wanted to go. Even Solomon Schultz, for all his loud arguing. And everyone in Schoenthal agreed that Canada was the place to go.

"And the Peter Harms family?" said Mother soberly.

Father looked back at her just as seriously. "That shall be as you decide, Sarah. You know that."

Father never tried to make up her mind for her—never once in all the weeks and months that followed. She knew well enough that he hoped and wished she would say yes. Other people did try to persuade her. Some parents came to say how much they wanted Teacher Harms to continue teaching their children. The people who attended the weekly Bible class were the most anxious of all. They needed Teacher Harms in Canada, they said.

Who would show them all the wonderful things in the Bible if he did not come with them?

Everyone else was beginning to prepare for the migration. The autumn rains had begun early this year. There was day after day of cold rainy weather, so that the harvesting was at a standstill. But in all the homes in Schoenthal fathers were building crates and boxes in which they would be packing household goods. Wherever you went you could hear saws and hammers going. Mothers were just as busy, spinning wool and cotton, and knitting stockings and underwear. The main topic of conversation was what they would pack for the long trip. How much clothing and bedding they would need. How much food and what kind. They need not worry about the sea voyage. The Canadian government would feed them on the ship. But before that, and after they landed in Canada, they would need to provide their own food.

Fathers talked about taking seedling fruit trees, and how one should pack them for the trip. They were planning to take seed grain too. They had to decide how much space all their goods would take, to make sure they had crates and boxes enough.

Only the Harmses were not doing a thing to get ready. School began, and Father taught each day. Since Agatha was gone, Cornelia had to help her mother more and more. Sometimes she grew hopeful. Mother was making pillows this fall— She didn't do that every year. But maybe she would have done it in any case. She had been saving goose feathers for several years.

The other children in school were buzzing with talk about the migration. It was like a contagious fever. All of Bergthal colony was moving, but not all at once. It was to be done in three stages, over three years. Each village must decide who would be going with the first group next spring.

And Mother still hadn't made up her mind.

Afterwards Cornelia used to wonder if she ever would have if it hadn't been for Aunt Gerda and Grandmother Siemens. They made a surprise visit to Schoenthal that autumn.

The rains had stopped, and now most days were sunny. But the roads were still muddy and no one expected visitors from far away Molotschna. Agatha certainly hadn't said a word about it in her last letter. All she ever wrote about was how good Wilhelm was to her, and how she got to boss the houseservants, and what a good manageress her mother-in-law said she was getting to be. Agatha seemed all Franz now.

This Friday evening Cornelia was setting the table for supper when she saw a carriage stopping beside the porch. Out stepped a familiar looking woman. Cornelia blinked in surprise.

"Grandmother!" she screamed. "Grandmother is here."

"Mother?" exclaimed mother, not believing. But then there was a race to see who could reach her first. Cornelia won. And for a minute nobody noticed the other passenger. Not until she spoke.

"Well! Peter! What's this I hear about you?"

"I can't imagine," said Peter Harms good-naturedly. "Come in, come in, Mother Siemens. To think that you would come to visit us this time of year. But you are heartily welcome. You too, Gerda."

Soberly Cornelia thought over his words. Grandmother couldn't have come without Aunt Gerda. And having Grandmother here was very unusual. Not in five years had she made the long trip. But Aunt Gerda was less welcome, at least to Cornelia. She could be counted on to make personal remarks.

And she did. About Cornelia—She *still* wasn't growing properly. What ever was the *matter*? About Bernhard—Poor boy. Poor, poor boy! He looked paler and weaker than ever. (Couldn't Aunt Gerda understand that it made your heart curl up with fear just to hear a thing like that?) About Johann and Anton— Now *there* were husky looking boys! They looked as if they'd be real men one of these days!

"But I hope," she said, turning to Father, "I hope you'll not be so foolish as to go off to far countries. I had hoped you had given up all that foolishness."

"Who mentioned anything about our going?" said Father.

"Cornelia," interrupted Mother, "cut some more spare ribs. And I'll slice more bread. The coffee is ready. Supper's ready. You two travellers will be ready for something to eat and for a hot drink."

"Yes, yes. Yes, yes," said Grandmother, beaming all around.

All throughout supper time she helped Cornelia's parents steer the conversation away from the migration. And afterwards the grownups went to the Big Room and closed the doors. So Cornelia washed the dishes, and Anton dried them. Bernhard sat behind the table, helping Johann with his arithmetic. The doors to the Big Room remained closed. Cornelia went to bed.

Next morning Aunt Gerda had a stunned look on her face. She spoke hardly one sentence thoughout breakfast time. The word migration wasn't mentioned. Not once.

And that noon, right after dinner, she and Grandmother drove away again.

Why? Why come at all if they hadn't meant to stay any longer? Cornelia felt all afternoon like— like a bottle of gooseberries that is fermenting! You can watch the bubbles forming, building up and up. And then, one day—BANG! The cork flies up, and the ceiling of the pantry is sprayed with gooseberries. That was exactly how she felt. If everybody kept acting so mysterious— If nobody would explain things soon, she'd explode.

She forced herself to walk into the kitchen quietly after school. She changed her apron. She washed her hands. She set the table. She got out the bread board and the big butcher knife.

"Well, Cornelia," said Mother casually, "are you ready to leave for Canada?"

Cornelia flashed around to look with wide eyes at her mother. "Are we going? Truly? How did you make up your mind?"

Father had come in. He looked at Mother too. His lips twitched, and then he and Mother both broke into laughter. At the sound all the boys came running, even Bernhard. They looked at Cornelia for an explanation. She shrugged her shoulders.

Mother, still giggling, wiped her eyes on her apron hem. "Your Aunt Gerda decided for me, I think."

"But she didn't *want* us to go!"

"I know." She and Father chuckled again.

Finally they sobered up enough to tell what happened behind the closed doors of the Big Room last night. Aunt Gerda had come all the way from Molotschna to tell her brother- and sister-in-law what they must do. It would be downright foolishness for them to go to Canada.

"You know how she is," said Mother.

Cornelia nodded soberly. "She makes you want to do exactly the opposite."

"So of course I answered boldly that I wanted to go," said Mother.

All the boys were grinning. Anton hopped around the room with excitement. Cornelia stood soberly pushing crumbs around on the bread board.

"Why, Cornelia! What happened? I thought you would be the most excited of all!"

"But if you said it only on account of Aunt Gerda—"

"I didn't." Mother began working briskly. She lifted some freshly churned butter, all dripping with buttermilk, out of the churn. She would wash and salt the rest after supper. She patted the sides of this bit smooth with a wooden spoon. She dipped soup out of the kettle. "I didn't. For days I have been thinking that it was God's will for us to go. That He wanted me to say yes. But— I dreaded leaving this country—my home country—and going out into a land which is strange to me. So I postponed and postponed my decision."

"And God sent Aunt Gerda to help you," said Johann.

"Very likely."

"What did Grandmother say?" asked Bernhard curiously.

Father and Mother were smiling at each other again.

"She surprised all of us," said Mother.

"She dumbfounded Gerda, I'm thinking," said Father with a chuckle.

Grandmother hadn't said a word, either for or against the Peter Harmses moving to Canada. Not until Sarah announced her decision. Then Grandmother smoothed her apron and exclaimed, *"Dauts gescheit!* (That's

69

sensible) And, Gerda, you may as well know now— I'm going with them."

Grandmother! Going to Canada? Openmouthed Cornelia stared at her parents. Delight dawned in her dark eyes. But then she thought of Aunt Gerda. Poor Aunt Gerda! For the first time in her life she felt sorry for her outspoken aunt. She brought Grandmother all the way hoping she would help her persuade the Harmses to stay in Russia. But that wasn't what Grandmother had in mind. She came to stiffen their backbones, she explained. And she was going home now to get ready for the trip next spring.

Now that her mind was made up, Sarah Harms set to work too. Peter Harms was, as she said, no good at building so much as a box. But the *Oberschulze* sent one of his servants who was good with hammer and saw. The upstairs storeroom became his workshop. It was filling up with boxes and crates, sawdust and chips. Sarah Harms began sorting through all the goods to determine which to take along to Canada, and what had better be sold here.

All around, the people were planning auction sales. Those who had few goods planned to lump their saleable goods together. Neighbors, Russians or German Lutherans, were coming to look at the houses. Schoenthal hardly seemed like home any more. So many strangers were streaming through, looking at all the houses and barns and fields.

Only on the hillside did one feel at home. Every fine evening and on Saturday afternoons it was covered with boys and girls, climbing, sliding and tumbling in the snow. The liveliest of them all was Cornelia. But every once in a while she would wave her wet mittened hand,

and an answering wave would come from the sunny side of a clump of brush at the foot of the hill. Bernhard never tried to climb the slope any more.

Puffing and redfaced she would join him later, and they would cross the bridge and walk home together slowly. The hill was one thing that Cornelia was sorry to leave behind.

When spring came the hillside was alive with tiny streams that fed into the river, the Bodena, which flowed into the Karatesch, then raced along to join the Berda. In school Teacher Harms was having a difficult time. Soon, soon the first group would be leaving, now that spring was here. It was like a fever in everyone's bloodstream.

There were conferences again in all the Mennonite colonies. Families were making up their minds. Were they going? Were they staying? *Oberschulze* Penner, who dropped in at Teacher Harmses one evening, announced, "The Czar is trying to stop the migration." Penner had just had a letter from the Chortitza colony and from the Molotschna.

"The Czar has sent his personal representative, Totleben, to visit the colonies and try to persuade the people to stay," he reported.

"But surely, he's too late!" exclaimed Father.

"He's a very friendly man and very persuasive, I've been told," said Penner, gloomily. "My latest word is that two thirds of those who at one time thought of going have decided to stay."

"And Bergthal?"

"Bergthal is going." The *Oberschulze* brought his hand down on the table with a slap. "Bergthal is going!

71

We are not among those who put our hands to the plough and then look back.''

That sounded fine and noble and exciting. But Cornelia could not feel sure that the Peter Harms family was actually going until Agatha and Wilhelm arrived, bringing Grandmother with them. Agatha had come for her final visit. Grandmother had brought all her personal goods, including the old seachest. — All the things that she meant to take with her to Canada!

IV
"Dear Agatha . . ."

"Cornelia! Up! Up!"

She sat up with a jerk, and looked about her sleepily. She had just dreamt that she was in Canada, surrounded by about forty Indians. But she was back in her little room in Schoenthal. Rain was pecking at the window panes. Daylight hadn't really arrived yet. Her father was looking in at her.

"Are you awake? Then get up. We must make an early start."

The last morning in Schoenthal. Quickly Cornelia slipped out of bed. Mother had laid clean clothes on the chair beside her. With eager fingers she dressed, tying a clean apron on last of all. Then she made a dash for the kitchen, and took the wooden comb out of its holder above the washstand.

For the last time. This was a strange thought. For the last time Cornelia would be combing her hair before this little mirror.

"Want me to do it?" asked Agatha.

In the year since her sister's marriage, Cornelia had learned to make neat braids. But—this would be the last time that Agatha could do it for her. Cornelia nodded and handed over the comb.

Wilhelm was outdoors, helping Teacher Harms rope the boxes and crates onto a wagon. Each crate had a card tacked to it saying,

PETER HARMS
MANITOBA, CANADA

We're going. We're going. Today we leave Schoenthal.
Cornelia hardly knew whether to laugh or to cry at the thought.

Mother, who had washed yesterday's clothes by hand late last night, was pressing and folding them. Grandmother was packing food for the trip. There were two large sackfuls of roasted buns. There was a smaller sackful of hard peppernuts. For today's lunches, Grandmother had fried *Rollkuchen* (crullers). Mrs. Jakob Penner, the wife of the *Oberschulze*, had sent over a basket of cherries and a pot of honey. They would go well with the crullers. The trip to the railway station at Nickolajowska would take all day. Forty miles to go! You had to plan for dinner and supper on the way. For later on there would be cheeses and a big boiled ham and *Speck* (bacon.)

This morning everyone had had breakfast except Cornelia, Johann and Anton. The boys, damp from the rain, their hair smelling like dog, came running in at Grandmother's call, just as Agatha finished Cornelia's braids.

"Eat, Children, eat!" advised Grandmother. "We must not keep the carriages waiting."

The boys gulped their milk and gobbled their bread and butter. Cornelia was almost too excited to swallow a mouthful. And she forgot about eating the moment Bernhard stuck his head into the kitchen.

"They're leaving! The wagons are leaving!" he called.

"Cornelia! Come back!" called Mother. "You'll catch a cold."

But Cornelia had raced out. She untied her apron and

put that over her head and shoulders like a cape. The main street of Schoenthal was filled with wagons and horses—one long irregular train of wagons and horses. Each was loaded high with boxes of varying sizes. Whole families perched on the crates, with baskets of food on their laps and blankets around their shoulders. The Schoenthalers who were not leaving yet stood in front of their picket gates, watching soberly.

Then came the crack of whips, and echoes skipping away among the treetops. "Hoa, hoa!" called the drivers. And the wagon train moved away.

"Child, child, what are you *thinking* of?" exclaimed Mother when Cornelia came running back into the kitchen. "What if you should catch a cold? Yes, you must eat something. You'll be very hungry before noon."

Agatha began washing the dishes. She and Wilhelm would be driving to Nickolajowska in their own carriage. They would be there when the train pulled away tomorrow. Cornelia had never seen a train. She had never seen a ship. She had never seen a tunnel. Father said that was a sort of hole that ran clear through a mountain. She would ride through the tunnels. She would see and experience many things. But—she might never see Agatha again.

"Cornelia, Cornelia, where are your thoughts?" asked Agatha gently. "Finish your breakfast."

Not once, since she came for a visit, had Agatha scolded Cornelia.

"Take." Cornelia pushed her cup and knife away. "I can't eat any more."

She needed to say goodbye. To the schoolroom. To every room in the house. To the shed where Brindle was still standing in her stall. Today she would go to the barn

75

of the *Oberschulze*. The Penners had bought her. She was a very good milker.

The *Oberschulze* would be staying in Schoenthal for two more years. He would stay to help wind up the business of the colony because he was such an important man. Then he would go to Canada with the last Bergthalers to seek a new home.

Cornelia stood in the low shed, patting Brindle's silky flank when she heard a sound. At first she thought it was the drip of rain from the eaves. But it wasn't. It was— Was someone *sobbing*? One window pane was broken. Johann did that last week with a ball. The sound seemed to come from the outside, through that opening. Cornelia peered through the window. Nothing. She opened the door, and peered round its edge. Someone was huddled against the wall. Rain dripped on him, and he was shaking with sobs.

"Hey! You! What's the matter?"

The boy raised a shaggy head. It was Daniel Martens. He was the Schoenthal boy who had seemed the most excited of all about going to Canada, especially since Bernhard was going too. They were best friends, even though Bernhard was short and slight, and Daniel was big for his age.

He had a sad life story. Nobody really knew who his parents were. Whoever they were, they hadn't wanted him. People whispered about it. He was a tiny day-old baby when a Schoenthal woman, Mrs. Martens, passed a pigpen and saw something wriggling in the muck. The sow might have trampled him into the muck. She might have gobbled him up! Someone had meant him to die. The bare thought made you shudder.

But Mrs. Martens came along in time. She wanted

76

him. She loved him as much as if he had been her own son. For a few years he had a good home. But then his foster mother died. The second Mrs. Martens wasn't nearly as kind.

"She told me—last night," said Daniel between heavy sobs—"That I—couldn't go—with them.— She said they— didn't have m-money— to th-throw away—on useless—trash—like me."

Cornelia didn't wait to hear any more. She ran into the kitchen. "Father—Father—" She tugged at his sleeve, her eyes flashing. "Come and see Daniel Martens." And she poured out the story he had told her.

"And he's still out in the rain? Why didn't you bring him in, child?"

She might have known Father would make Daniel's troubles his own.

Two carriages waited before the door—Wilhelm's and the *Oberchulze's*. Mr. Penner himself meant to take the Harms family all the way to the train station. Wilhelm would be taking Grandmother Siemens and three old Schoenthal ladies. The horses were pawing the ground with impatience. But they had to wait while the teacher called the *Oberschulze*, and together they listened to Daniel's story.

Mr. Penner's face grew red with anger. It was a shame—a shame! he said. Nobody in the Bergthal colony had to stay behind because he was too poor. Daniel had as much right to go to Canada as anyone!

"And you're going! Stay with me until we leave, boy. I'll see to it that you get your rights."

So one of the last things the Harmses saw was Daniel waving quite cheerfully as they drove away. In a short time they had caught up with the mile-and-a-half long train of wagons. Not all came from Schoenthal. There were emigrants from every Bergthal village, all going to Nickolajowska together. It was safer so, on account of robbers. The rain was only drizzling now, which was a good thing. A forty mile wagon ride in rain would be a very cold and clammy experience.

Even going by closed carriage it was late afternoon before the Harmses reached Nickolajowska. Here Father became the pilot. The two carriage loads would be spending the night with the Nels Zimmermanns. Mr. Zimmermann was a teacher-friend of Peter Harms's. The train wasn't leaving until four o'clock Sunday afternoon. Tomorrow.

On that tomorrow the station was crowded with people. Hundreds of people. Hundreds of boxes had been loaded onto the freight cars. And now it was the people's turn. Father was having a long handshake with the *Oberschulze* and with Wilhelm. Cornelia was looking for Agatha, but she couldn't see her clearly. Mother was hugging and kissing Agatha. Then Cornelia felt a pair of arms go around her. They squeezed, hard.

"Be sure to write me. Write everything that happens," said Agatha. "Do you hear?"

"Yes," agreed Cornelia breathlessly. "I will. *Aufwiedersehen! Aufwiedersehen!*" (Till we meet again)

Inside the train car she looked through grimy windows to where Agatha stood beside Wilhelm, clinging to his hand. She looked lonesome there.

Hamburg, Sunday, June 23—or July 5
"Dear Agatha,
"Isn't it funny? Father says that now that we are away from Russia we must get used to a different sort of calendar. You have to add 12 days to the old one. So it's

78

actually July 5 where we are. *Why* is that? Do you know?

It seems strange to think that it is a week since we said goodbye at Nickolajowska. Agatha, we changed trains, *and changed trains*! We travelled on six different trains. And part of the time two long trains were coupled together. All full of emigrants. We went through two long tunnels, too. It's very dark in a tunnel, and it smells of coal gas, so you almost have to choke. Father says this is because the smoke from the engine cannot escape into the outside air.

It took us six days to reach Hamburg. We got here at 4 o'clock in the morning yesterday. We are staying in the Tehrhof now. It is a big building, like six large houses piled one on top of the other. Here we wait for a steamship to take us to England.

Agatha, something sad happened on the way. Two babies died. In the same night. I was sorry for the mothers. I must close now. Mother and Grandmother are getting supper ready. Father bought some raspberries yesterday. We have some cheese and a bit of ham left. Grandmother says we might as well eat it all, because when we travel by ship we will not eat our own food, and it would spoil.

The Tehrhof is crowded. It's hard to sleep here, because there are so many babies crying, and little children running around, and mothers calling their children. We are glad Grandmother is going to Canada with us. Especially Mother. But I am very glad too. Your loving, only sister,

Cornelia

Liverpool, England—Sunday, June 30—or July 12

Dear Agatha,

Isn't Liverpool a funny name. I wonder who would choose a name like that. It doesn't sound pretty—and it isn't a pretty place. Because of the smoke. But the harbour is big, and there are many ships, big and little. The ship whistles are deep and hollow sounding. They send funny shivers up and down your back. Not from fear. It's a strange feeling.

But I must tell you about the ship and the train. We left Hamburg on Tuesday. That's five days ago. First we steamed down the Elbe. The river is wide, wide, and we passed many ships. The emigrants could not all go on the same ship. Oh, my no! We went on a freighter, and Father said this was a good thing for us because there weren't many cabins, but they were nice. Not so crowded. And the food was very good.

Once we thought Anton was lost, and we got scared. Maybe he had fallen overboard! But after a bit a sailor brought him. Do you know where the *Schelm* (rascal) had been? He went down into the hold of the ship. It was full of cattle. They were being taken to England to be butchered.

When we sailed into the North Sea there was an accident. In the dark near us two ships rammed each other. They were close enough so we could hear shouts and groans. I was on deck with Father and Bernhard.

Bernhard is enjoying the trip. He didn't get the least bit seasick when we had stormy weather. All the rest of us did. But I missed only one meal.

The place we landed was called Grimsby. That's on the east side of England. About in the middle. We got there at 11 o'clock. All of us had to go into a building where

80

they asked a lot of questions about us, and about our boxes and things. Where were we going and everything— They wanted to know it all. Did I tell you? Father has been studying English! He could talk with the men a little. I think English sounds very funny.

At two o'clock we boarded a train to cross England. It took seven hours, and the trains here go very fast. Much faster than in Russia and Germany. This is the country where Queen Victoria lives. She will be our queen when we get to Canada, too. That seems funny, but it is true. She is a very great queen, over many lands all over the world, Father says.

On the way to Liverpool we saw many interesting things—high bridges and villages and green fields. But we saw much smoke, too. Father says there are three manufacturing cities close together. I don't remember the names. We went through tunnels, too, but now we weren't so much afraid of them. But we were frightened when we got to Liverpool station. Ach, the noise! The confusion! People running this way, that way. Trains whistling and shrieking. They were racing forward, and racing backward again. Grandmother said it made her think of the great day of judgment.

Now we are waiting for our ship to take us to Canada.

What do you think? Father has had to spank Anton two times. Because he always runs away. He is so curious. Father says curiosity killed the cat. Which cat did he mean? I get tired of running after Anton all the time to make sure he is not getting into mischief or danger.   Cornelia

On the ship "Laconia," Monday, July 8—or 20
    Dear Agatha,
    I wanted to write you yesterday, but it was too

stormy. We have had much stormy weather. Ach! So stormy that everybody was sick. Except Bernhard. The waves went so high they struck the basket on the masts. That's forty feet above the top deck, Father says.

There are curved pipes on deck. They are for ventilation. But the water from the waves slammed right into the pipes and down into the hold. It washed on deck too, and down the stairs. We had to walk *patch-patch* in water, like geese. Many of us immigrants sleep on mattresses on the floor. At first when the ship began rocking, the mattresses slipped and slipped. Sometimes our heads slammed against one wall. Sometimes our feet slammed against the opposite wall. *Ach, du mein!* It makes you very sorry that you ate any supper.

But when the water came rushing down the stairs, that was worst of all. It soaked into the mattresses. So all the men began carrying the water up. We girls helped to scoop it up into pails. The men had to climb two long flights of stairs. And all the time the stairs and the railings and walls were tilting, this way, that way. It was crazy. I was so afraid Father would fall down and get hurt.

Tell Martha that when you sail away from a land, all the time the land seems to be sinking into the ocean. That's because the world is round. We could see the mountain peaks of Ireland for two days.

I hope it will stay calm now till we get to Canada.

Your loving little sister,
Cornelia

On the "Laconia", Monday, July 15—or 27
    Dear Agatha,
    We're *still* on the ship. Maybe that's on account of the icebergs!

Friday was an exciting day. It was *cold.* In *July!* So cold that everybody who had a coat put it on. The air got foggier and foggier. I was on the second class deck with Father. We were looking for Anton again. We saw two seamen staring and staring into the fog. Then one yelled up at the Captain. He was standing by the big wheel. He turned and turned the wheel, and slowly began backing up. But a big frightening white mountain came swimming out of the fog. Ooh, it was dreadful. And beautiful. It bumped the ship. A moment before, Father had grabbed Anton and me, and pulled us to the other side of the deck. So when the ice crashed down on the deck no one was hurt. But the iron railing was bent, and the wooden hull outside the rails was smashed to bits.

Sailors cleared the ice away. But for a long time the ship didn't move. The ice mountain gradually slipped away into the fog again. So then the engines began again, and we went forward slowly. Father said it was a good thing the sailors dropped the anchors before we hit the icebergs. The ship could have been smashed, and there'd be no Cornelia to write you about it.

After the fog lifted all the Bergthalers got together and we sang songs of thanksgiving. We sang, "Now thank we all our God." And *"Groszer Gott, wir loben Dich."* It was like a Sunday church meeting. Because God had kept us all from drowning.

The next day we came to St. John's, Newfoundland. The morning sun shone nicely—but then it got foggy again. I was afraid. We saw many icebergs, and we moved along very slowly. Twice we stopped altogether. Just stopped, with a ring of ice-bergs staring at us! We waited for them to drift apart.

On Friday a baby died. Peter Friesen's little girl. One

hour later, do you know what they did? They let her body sink into the ocean. And then we came to the city of Halifax. That's part of Canada! The name sounds funny, not?

We stayed in Halifax harbour all day. Men were unloading and loading bales and boxes and crates. Next day we sailed on, and the weather was stormy again. It was Sunday, but everyone was too sick. We didn't have any meeting. So we had it today.

What do you think? We can see land ahead. And that is where we are going to land. Soon now. Your little sister,
Cornelia

Dear Agatha and Wilhelm,

Mother says I shall write you a letter, too. It is hard work. At Liverpool we got on the ship. We got on the ship in the morning. For dinner we had flour soup and bread and butter. The soup didn't taste very good. Some people grumbled. But a man said we should wait—tomorrow we would all be satisfied. With the food. Father said that was a joke. Tomorrow we were seasick. Nobody ate. It's a very bad feeling to be seasick.

I saw the anchors come out of the water. There is a big wheel in the back part of the ship. And 12 men put twelve poles into holes in the wheel. They walked round and round. And they sang. Hey he, hallada, falladra, falladra. They sang other words too. But the falladra thing was the chorus. That is what Father says. The rope came up wet. It wrapped around the thick pole at the centre of the wheel. Then the anchors came up. That was so we could sail.

But before that I saw something else. I saw old Mr. Thielmann get almost drowned. He is blind. And his grandson, Heinrich, was leading him. All of us had to walk up some boards to get into the ship. Mr. Thielmann was carrying a bag of roasted buns. He fell in, and the buns fell too. The buns floated. Mr. Thielmann didn't. But he held on to the buns. So the two sailors knew where to fish for him. This is a true story. They fished Mr. Thielmann out of the water. But the buns they had to throw away. They were all wet and salty.

Soon we will be in Canada.

Your brother, Johann

Immigration house, Quebec, Tuesday, July 16—or 28

Dear Agatha,

Most of us were asleep when the ship came to Quebec. It was 11 o'clock. When I awoke this morning the ship was hardly rocking at all. Everyone was scrambling around because we were going on shore. The sea voyage is over. Just think of that! We are on the other side of the world. All the mothers were worried about their children. We had to get washed and combed and eat breakfast. And then we began to land. We are staying in a big immigration house now. I must close. Father and Mother want to take us for a walk!

Your sister,
Cornelia

Later:

Oh, Agatha, Canada is beautiful! On our walk we saw a high cliff, with trees growing on the top. And there was a river that ran at the foot of the cliff. And the air was full of the smell of flowers. Tomorrow early, at 4 o'clock, we must board a train.

Collingwood, Ontario, Canada. Monday, July 22—or Aug. 3

Dear Agatha,

We are in an immigration house, waiting for a steamship again. We have been riding trains and riding trains. Three trains. And three more children have died, too. Sunday there was a funeral for two children. I am tired of funerals.

Moorhead, Minnesota, United States of America—Tuesday, July 30—or Aug. 11

Dear Agatha,

Guess where I am sitting. On a grassy bank, beside the Red River. We are living in tents—a whole city of tents. Like the children of Israel in the Bible. All of us are camping here. We are waiting for our last boat. It will take us right to the place where our land waits for us.

We sailed and we sailed, over two of the biggest lakes in the world. The Superior is the biggest lake that has fresh water. And the Huron is the third biggest. Between the two there are locks. But Johann says I must not tell you about them. He wants to.

Agatha, another baby died. One was born, too, but I am tired of funerals. The day the baby died the ship stopped for a little while at a town—and the parents had to give their dead baby to strangers for them to bury.

The ship arrived here in Moorhead at seven o'clock on Sunday morning.

Later: We have been waiting here for two days now. All the crates and boxes have been loaded onto a flat boat, called a barge. It has no engine. The boat, when it comes, will pull the barge—or maybe push it.

Dear Agatha and Wilhelm,

Cornelia is mean. She wants to write all the interesting parts. But I wouldn't let her. This is a boy's matter. It's all about engineering. Girls can't be engineers.

86

At one place a big lake used to flow into another big one. One lake was higher than the other, so there were water falls between. Now there is a water ladder. That is what Father calls it. But I think it's more like big stone rooms, with gates at both ends of the rooms. But there is no roof overhead. Only the sky. One room leads to the next. And that one leads to the next. If you want to go down the ladder, your ship sails into the first room. The gates are locked. Tight. Then an engine pumps water out of the room. And the water sinks, and the walls rise higher and higher.

When the water is low enough. The next gate opens. And the ship sails into that room. Finally the ship gets to the bottom of the ladder. And there you are. On the second big lake. Superior is the biggest lake and the best lake. In the world. Half of it belongs to Canada. How do you measure half a lake, Wilhelm? I want to know. Pretty soon we will be in Canada. Now we are living in tents. Like Indians.

Johann Harms

Rat River Landing, Manitoba, Canada. Sunday, Aug. 11—or 23

Dear Agatha,

We are living in immigration sheds now. There are four sheds, all alike. When the sun shines the place is all right. When it rains the roof leaks, and our bedding gets wet. Just now it is raining. And I am sitting under a table, so the paper will not get wet!

We have no floors but the grass. So even if there are many people coming and going, their footsteps are not noisy. But there is much talking, much planning. Many fathers are going out every day to look at land and to decide where they will be living. In the evenings there is talk about which families will be going together to form a village. Sometimes there are loud arguments. Some mothers have said that the *Oberschulze* should be here! He would set things right!

But I want to tell you about how we got here from Moorhead.

We got tired of waiting for a boat. But Father says the town of Moorhead got tired of having so many immigrants sitting on the river bank so long, too. He read a paper that said, "We have Mennonites for breakfast, Mennonites for dinner, Mennonites for supper." Father and Bernhard thought that was very funny. But Grandmother said they should be glad for the immigrants. Those that had money bought a lot of food there. We got very tired of eating roasted buns all the time. There is a cookstove here, in the middle room, which is the kitchen. Mother can cook good things for us again. That is nice.

Because the steamer was so slow in coming, we and some other families left Moorhead on the barge. There was no engine at all. There were no rooms either, so we slept out of doors that night. We drifted down the river. The bargemen had long poles to keep us away from the banks.

It was interesting. So quiet. For a whole day we just went drifting along. The banks were covered with trees and bushes. Sometimes we saw berries, and the bargemen let us land and pick our aprons full. But the second day the steamer caught up with us. The barge was attached to the steamer. We went faster then.

I was glad that we could stay on the barge. On account of Bernhard, and on account of myself too. Once I went into the cabins on the steamer. Phui! There was hardly any air at all! I don't know how they could breathe in there. But we had more mosquitoes during the night. They are real pests. The bargemen made smoke in two pails so the little tormentors could not bite us so much. But I am all lumpy.

We stopped at many places along the river. At each landing there were barrels and boxes waiting to be picked up. We saw many Indians, too. They didn't hurt us at all. But their faces are closed. They look as if they have deep secret thoughts. I wonder— Are they friendly thoughts?

There were Indians waiting for us when we landed. Half-Indians, Father says. They were partly French, and very dark skinned. Mr. Hespeler had hired them and their wagons to take us to the immigration sheds, five miles away. Do you remember Mr. Hespeler? He is the German-Canadian who made the arrangements so we could come to Canada. He is very much interested in the Mennonite immigrants.

Because it was Saturday evening when we landed— and that's a week ago yesterday—we hurried to get here before night came. The wagons took the people first, then went back for all the boxes and trunks and things.

Something funny happened on the way. We came to a place where the land was low and wet. The drivers made motions that all the men and boys should get off and walk. And oh, Agatha, I think Bernhard should not have done it. He has a bad cold now. But he laughed hardest of all when the funny thing happened.

The oxen walked very slowly. And at that place they had to pull the wagons through water and mud. They went so slow, it seemed they might stop, and the wagons sink deep into the mud. So the men and boys took off their hats, and they yelled, "Hoa! Hoa!"

Do you know what, Agatha? The oxen stopped! In this country you say "Hoa, hoa!" when you mean "Pr-r-r-r!" Funny, not?

Father and Bernhard knew this. But the other men couldn't know why the drivers got so angry.

It took a long while to get the whole wagon train moving again. So it was late before we arrived at the sheds. (This place is called Schanzenberg, because Mr. Jakob Shantz of Ontario built it for immigrants. And because there is a hill a quarter mile north of this place.) And then we had to choose our rooms, and arrange the sleeping. And then the mothers had to get the supper ready. It was late, late before we went to sleep.

Yesterday another group of immigrants arrived here. We will soon have to move out to make room for the new ones that keep coming. I asked—and do you know, Agatha, in every group there have been people dying, dying. Those who came yesterday brought two dead bodies with them. They died on the Red River steamer. One old grandmother and a little boy. There is a new graveyard on that hill north of here now. Today there was a double funeral.

So now we are in Canada. Schoenthal seems very far away. It is a strange feeling not to have a home. Will we be glad that we came?

Your loving sister,
Cornelia

Aug. 16—or 28
Dear children, Agatha and Wilhelm,

Greetings of love. Since our last letters so much has happened. Grandmother Siemens stood the trip remarkably well, and except for Bernhard all of us seem to be well. He caught a heavy cold, and we cannot help fearing that this will be too much for his weakened constitution. We must face the possibility that God will take him away from us soon. Bernhard is ready. His heart rests peacefully in his Savior's love—and our hearts are at peace about him. But we fear for Cornelia. She has always had a special love for her older brother. How she will bear the parting, if it comes, we do not know.

I have chosen my 160 acres of land. It will not be part of a village tract, for various reasons, which I will explain in my next letter. I have been asked to teach the Schoenfeld village school. (They will be mostly Schoenthal people living there.) So for this coming winter we will be living in the village. In spring each father will plough one acre of land for me. And they will give me $65.00 for the winter, besides. This in return for teaching their children. It was decided at the last *Schulzenbott*.

It is late in the year, and much needs to be done before winter sets in. I am told the winters here can be very grim.

Later. Sunday night, Aug. 18—or 30

It has pleased the Lord to take our dear Bernhard to Himself. He died at 7:28 tonight. There was a meeting in one of the immigration sheds, so this one was quiet and deserted, except for us. Bernhard died peacefully and gently as he lived.

Our hearts are sad as yours will be. But is not the Lord the God of all comfort? He will know how to apply the healing balm. I commend you especially, Agatha, to Him at this hour.

Did our emigrating hasten his death? I hardly think so. The best doctors told me that he had little time left in this world—and also that a sea voyage might be good for him. He has been a great joy to us all the way.

Your loving father,
Peter Harms

Tuesday, Aug. 20—or Sept. 1

Dear Agatha,

Mother says I shall write you a letter. We have sunny weather now. But winter is coming. We must get our homes built. We will live in Schoenfeld village. The fathers will build the schoolhouse first, they say. That is where we will live this winter. Bernhard is dead.

Cornelia

V
Homesteaders

There was a constant coming and going in the Schanz shelters now. Every week or so more immigrants arrived. Every week those who had stayed in the sheds for a week or two or three, moved on to their chosen land. There was a lot of dying too—and of being born. More and more graves were dug on the ridge a quarter mile north of the sheds. And now and then you could hear the first angry crying of a new-born, red-faced baby.

The Peter Harms family would have to move out soon. But first they planned to go down the Red River to Winnipeg. It was high time. They needed farm tools. And household things. And groceries. But during the night before they were to leave, a baby was born in the crowded little room next to theirs. The family had just arrived that very day. The name was Driedger, and there were' three little children who were still cranky and tired from the long, long journey.

Cornelia's mother went to help when the baby was about to be born. Cornelia herself didn't notice a thing until she heard the whispers early that morning as she lay on her hay mattress. Everybody whispered in the Schanz sheds. Unless they did not mind being overheard by a dozen other families.

"I'll simply have to stay," whispered Mother. "There is no one here to take care of the poor things."

And Father whispered back, "Couldn't Driedger himself take care of things?"

"He? He's perfectly useless in a sickroom. As helpless as an infant. No, someone will need to take charge. And all the other women have their hands full. Mine—mine are empty."

There was a little silence. *Empty. Because of Bernhard,* thought Cornelia. She thought of him first thing every morning, last thing every night. *He's dead— dead—dead.* But it still did not seem true.

Mother was whispering again. "And I think Cornelia had better stay to keep the older three children occupied."

"Not Cornelia." Father felt so strongly about it, he said the words aloud.

"Peter's right," said Grandmother. "I will stay and help you with the family, Sarah. Cornelia needs to go."

On account of Bernhard, thought Cornelia again. But it didn't matter. Nothing mattered very much since she had lost her brother. Nothing. Not coming to a new country. Not the chance to see and experience new things. Not the new home they would soon be going to. With Bernhard all this would have been exciting fun. Without him the whole world seemed to be crying, even when the sun shone. But she hadn't cried. Not a single tear.

"Cornelia?" called Mother. Not in a whisper now. The whole Schanz shed was astir. Babies were bawling. Older children were fretting or squealing with laughter. Mothers were scolding.

"Cornelia? Up. I need your help."

She dressed quickly, all but her feet. Barefooted, she ran outdoors to the box where the tin basins stood in a row. There was a smoothly rounded cake of yellow soap. Cornelia dipped a cupful or two of river water out of a barrel, and scrubbed her face and hands. The water was cold, and the grass was cold and wet under her feet. She raced back and forth a few times to wash her feet in the dewy grass. This was better than using water for the job. You had to be saving with water.

All the water for the washing and cooking and drinking needs had to be hauled by oxcart from the river five miles away. Five hours, going and coming. Several oxcarts did nothing all day but haul water, and haul water.

Father said that one of the things that had to be done—and soon—was to dig a well here. So the oxcarts could have a rest for a change. And so there would always be enough water for everyone.

There was another matter, something that wasn't nice to talk about. *Lice.* During the long trip almost everyone had picked up lice. It couldn't be helped. People lived too close together, with too little chance for cleanliness. Once they lived on their own place—*how* Mother would boil and boil their clothes! And how she would scrub and scrub their heads. Those pesky things would just *have* to go!

Their land had water enough, that was one cheering thing. Father chose it partly for that very reason. A creek ran across one corner, and as long as the weather remained mild enough, they meant to live in a tent on their land. When real winter weather came, Father said, they would have to move into the schoolhouse.

But until then we'll live like Indians, thought Cornelia with a flash of joy. At one place along the Red River she and Bernhard had seen an encampment of about thirty skin tents in one cluster. *She and Bernhard.* The flash died as quickly as it came. Bernhard wasn't here. What was the use of anything without him?

He would have enjoyed the trip to Winnipeg. The banks were steep and covered with trees. You could see squirrels and chipmunks. Now and then you could even hear a bird call, in spite of the engine of the steamer and its screaming whistle at every bend of the river.

Father had intended to hire a canoe and an Indian canoeist to take them to the city. But a river steamer came round the bend just as he and the three children reached the landing after their five-mile walk. It was pushing a barge. That was loaded with goods, but there was room enough for a few passengers to ride safely, and the bargemen didn't mind.

English speaking ladies leaned over the railing of the boat, looking down at Cornelia, smiling and making motions.

"Look at her! Look at her! Isn't she quaint? With that basket over her arm . . . Like a Dutch painting."

What was "quaint"? What was "basket"? What was "Dutch painting"? "Look at her" Cornelia understood. It did not seem very polite to stare at her like that. Now they were making motions that Cornelia should come on board the boat.

"Want to?" said Father.

Cornelia shook her head.

"Thank you," called Father carefully in English, "She does—not—want—to, please."

Anton and Johann were clambering over the crates, or chasing one another around them. Cornelia chose a crate to perch on. Her shoes, joined by their laces, were draped over her apron belt. Her bare feet felt the rough lumber under her soles. The warmth and roughness were comforting. Dreamily her eyes watched the treetops glide past. If only, only Bernhard were here . . . .

96

"What are you thinking about?" Father had taken a seat beside her.

Cornelia couldn't say it. The words refused to come.

He guessed it anyway. "About Bernhard," he said.

She nodded.

"Where is your brother now? Do you think about that?"

Her eyes were dry and burning. "In the grave," she said.

"Is he? Listen, Cornelia. 'I am the resurrection and the life. He that believeth in me, though he were dead, yet shall he live.' Do you remember who said that?"

"Jesus."

"Yes, Jesus. Can you not trust His word? Bernhard did. He believed—and he is not dead. He is alive, and in a much better place. He cannot come back to us—but we can go to him. If his Saviour is our Saviour, too."

Father went to round up the boys then. The sun was directly overhead, and it was time to unpack the basket. Mother had packed freshly baked *Schnettke* (biscuits) and a jar of honey, and a stone jug of cold coffee. They ate as they watched the farmsteads glide past. It seemed as if most farmyards were laid along the river. That must be on account of the water. It was the farmers' highway, and it sustained their lives.

The sun was beginning to set when the steamer nudged the pier at the Winnipeg landing. Bargemen slid some planks across to the bank. Cornelia and her brothers ran nimbly across. They were waiting for their father who came more slowly, when the two ladies who had spoken to Cornelia earlier stopped beside her on the pathway. One was carrying some oranges and cookies. She held them out to Cornelia with a smile.

"These—are—for—you," she said clearly and slowly.

Father spoke up quietly behind Cornelia. "Say 'thank you'."

Cornelia blushed. "*Dankeschoen*, Madame," she said, with a curtsey.

"Ah! Charming!" exclaimed the second lady.

"*Sehr nett!* (very nice)" said the lady of the oranges, her eyes laughing. And they went on up the street. A sign read: Postoffice Street.

"This is where we must go, too," said Father. "Davis Hotel is just at the end of this streeet, on the other side of the road." One of the men at the Schanz shelters had told him about the place.

And he had been right. There was the hotel. On the way, the Harmses stopped at a little store where Father bought some sausages and buns. In their hotel room they ate supper, finishing with one cookie and one orange each. The fruit was still strange and interesting to them. Never in Russia had they seen any oranges.

After supper they lay down to sleep. It wasn't easy to drop off. There was a lot of noise downstairs and in the hall. But finally Cornelia must have dozed off, because when she opened her eyes it was morning.

Breakfast at the hotel was strange too. *Gruetze* (oatmeal), and thick pancakes, and fried potatoes, and flat pieces of fried meat called beefsteak. For breakfast! Cornelia felt strange enough to be eating at a long table with people who spoke a strange language. Father used all the English he knew and learned a few more new words. Everybody was friendly to the boys and to him. They smiled as they watched Johann and Anton eating. The two were filling up as if they expected this to be their last chance to eat.

After breakfast began the business of the day. The children followed their father from store to store. Mother had sent a shopping list. Father had one of his own. An axe, a shovel, a hay fork, a spade, a saw . . . One dollar . . one dollar . . . one dollar . . . The dollars were melting away very fast. Cornelia was relieved to notice that the coffee mill mother wanted cost only fifty cents. Soap was twenty five cents. (But Mother would be making her own as soon as she had some fat and wood ashes collected.) Matches were thirty cents. Dried apples were twelve cents a pound, white loaf sugar was twenty cents.

Cornelia tugged at her father's sleeve. "The yellow is two cents less," she whispered.

"Does Mother use that in cooking?"

"Oh, yes!"

"Well, I think I had better take some of both." The groceries they were buying today would have to last till spring. So Father bought six bags of flour. And a small wooden barrel of salted herring. And a large barrel containing a whole pickled pig! He bought a big ham, and several large pieces of dried beef. And a big crockful of lard.

"What else do we need?"

"Shoes for Anton and Johann," whispered Cornelia. She could not help whispering today. Wherever they went, people said the word "Mennonite", and they nodded at the Harmses and laughed. It was not a happy experience.

In the end, Father bought shoes and overshoes for all four of them. The overshoes smelled of rubber and had buckles. Next they bought two stoves, a small heater, and a large cookstove. They cost forty dollars! Father also bought some pots and kettles, and that was another three dollars and fifty cents.

"Now, is there anything you would like for yourself, Cornelia?" said Father. "Some peaches, perhaps?"

She had been looking at them, her mouth watering. Plump fuzzy peaches, pink and yellow in colour—just like in Russia. But they cost fifteen cents per pound!

"One for each of us," decided Father. "To take home with us, as a special treat."

Then Father got out his bag of money and he and the storeman began figuring out what their bill was in golden roubles. There had to be enough left over for a span of oxen and a wagon. Father hoped they could drive all the way home and save the freight.

He had bought a newspaper. They still had some sausage and buns left, a few cookies and two oranges. So they went down to the river bank and sat in the grass to eat. Then Father slowly spelled through the page where oxen were for sale. They had to ask directions to the place. It happened to be close to the river, not far at all for a walk. First they saw a long barn. Several men and boys stood around, or sat on rail fences. There were other people looking over the teams, some of horses, some oxen.

"Why don't we buy horses?" said Johann eagerly. "Why not, Father?·They go faster. And they look nicer. Why not, Father?"

There was a handsome team of bays, and Johann's eyes sparkled. He had learned a good deal about horses from Wilhelm.

Father didn't know a lot about either horses or oxen. But he knew the answer to Johann's questions.

"Because horses need some grain in their feed. And all

we'll have this winter is hay. Oxen are cheaper to feed."

"Want I should yoke the oxen for you?" asked one man.

Oxen. That sounded almost like the German name. And was *yoke* the same as *Joch*? It must be. Because the man brought out a flat board with two hollows cut out along one edge of it. The board fitted over the necks of the team. He attached lines to the board, and again to the wagon. Father was excited as he climbed to the seat.

"Want to give your young'uns a ride?" said the man.

"Wollt ihr mit?" called Father. ("Do you want to come along?")

The boys were up beside him instantly. Cornelia shook her head, crowding up against the fence corner. The man started the team, and Father drove slowly around the yard. Then he wanted to go faster. He slapped the reins. "Hoa! Hoa!" he called.

And the oxen stood.

Cornelia laughed. She remembered the time when the long train of oxcarts got stuck in the mud on the way to the Schanz shelters. She remembered how she and Bernhard laughed, and couldn't stop laughing. And suddenly now she found herself crying. She didn't want to cry. She was ashamed. What would the strangers think of her, a great big girl of twelve, crying. For no reason at all! She couldn't stop.

Father was beside her.

"Ishesick? Ishesick?" the man kept asking. ("Is she sick?") It was a question, but Cornelia couldn't understand what it meant.

"Come, Cornelia. Come boys. Let's walk down to the water," said Father.

101

"Don't you want the team?" called the man, sounding disappointed.

"Another time, maybe," said Father.

Cornelia was glad to get to a private place on the river bank. Tears were still dripping from her eyes.

"I don't know why! I don't know why!" she said, bewildered.

"Cry, cry," said Father soothingly. "These are healing tears. Now the first soreness because of Bernhard can be washed away."

He wrapped his coat around her because she had begun to shiver. He and the boys went down to the water, to wade, and to toss stones. After a while Cornelia slept.

"Feel better now?"

Cornelia had opened her eyes. The lids felt stiff and swollen. Her head felt stuffed. Even her tongue was stiff. And the hollows of her eyes ached. But her heart—she thought dreamily—her heart was like the "Laconia," floating on a calm sea after days and days of storm. She smiled slowly in response to her Father's anxious smile.

That moment she heard a sound. All of them heard it. A long, wailing, screeching sound. You couldn't tell at first from where it came. The whole world seemed to be full of the sound.

"There! Look!" said Father, pointing westward, to where the sun was setting. Against the red light they saw dark carts moving, two-wheeled carts pulled by oxen, a long, slow, protesting train of carts.

"Furs," said Father, looking excited. "They're bringing furs from the North West Territories."

Just like in the story books, thought Cornelia. This was like being part of one of the adventure stories that Father often told.

He didn't buy the oxen after all. He said he had thought better of the whole thing. Other farmers were buying them now to use them in winter for hauling logs home. But he would be busy in school. The Schoenfeld farmers were going to plough his land in spring. So he wouldn't need a team yet. And he wouldn't need hay, except for a cow. If he could find a good one. He did buy a tent though—an Indian tent, made of skins.

There was a barge waiting to go up river again. Father hired a dray wagon to take all the goods down to the barge landing. And after another night in the hotel, and another strange Canadian breakfast, the Harmses were on their way again. They travelled faster than they would have by oxcart. But at the Schanz landing, Peter Harms had to hire an oxteam to take the goods to the shelters. The four of them preferred to walk. It was quicker.

Mother had supper waiting. It was the happiest meal the family had had since Bernhard died. Perhaps not exactly happy. Peaceful. Relaxed. They decided to move out to their own land the very next morning. When the wagon-load of goods arrived, Father did not unload them. He hired the same driver, a Metis, to take the family to its new home. They added a few trunks and crates, and roped them down.

"But who'll guard the things this night?"

"In Canada you don't have to guard your things," said Father. "Isn't that right?" he called out to several men.

"That's right, that's really right," they answered. "In Canada we need not be afraid of robbers. This is a free country."

And when the Harms family came out of the shelter the next morning, not a thing was missing. Grandmother shook her head in wonder.

They were astir early, but softly so as not to awaken the neighbours. The grass was crisp with hoarfrost, so everyone wore shoes for the walk. Grandmother and Mother rode on the wagon seat. The driver stood behind them.

"Giddap," he grunted, and he cracked his whip.

"What would Aunt Gerda say?" said Cornelia.

"To what? To what?" her brothers wanted to know.

"Mother and Grandmother driving away with one of those wild Indians, one of those people eaters!"

They laughed, and they waved as they laughed. Then the four of them began walking. "We'll get there first," boasted Anton.

"It would be a shame if we didn't," said Father. "Think of the load the oxen are drawing."

Cornelia thought she would have liked to walk to the ridge where Bernhard was buried. Just once. Sort of saying goodbye. But she felt too shy to ask Father. It was a strange thing. Until now they had not been able to coax her to come with them when they went. She felt different today.

The flat and empty land was covered with frosted grasses. When the sun arose, the footing became very slippery. Trudging along, Cornelia thought of these past weeks. She was in Manitoba, Canada. In the place where she and Bernhard had often dreamed of being. There was the splendid sun, shining on a silvery sea of grass. There were clumps of trees, all silvered too. But farther away were some clusters of brown heaps.

"Father, what are those? Over there, can you see? Brown, like long stacks—old, old hay, or something.

"Those are villages. That's Heuboden. That's Gruenfeld."

104

Puffing from their scrambling walk, the boys stopped to stare.

"But—but where are the *houses*? Where are the *trees*?"

"Trees!" Father laughed. "Give them time to grow, boys."

He explained that with winter coming there wasn't time to build real homes. Almost all the immigrants planned to live in sod homes, called *simlins*. First you dug a shallow rectangular cellar hole, about three feet deep. Then you cut sods, and used them to build low walls around the cellars. Then you put a roof over it all—and there was your home.

"I'll take you to see them at work," promised Father.

When they tired of walking they sat down for a few minutes and ate a slice of bread and butter each. The grass was too damp for a comfortable seat, though, so the rest was brief. About half-past ten Father identified the stake that told where their land began. He made a sweeping motion with his arm. *There it is. That's our land*, it said elatedly.

It was an elated feeling. But a bit frightening too. Father had never been a farmer. He and they all would have to learn many new things in this new country. Who was going to teach them?

Cornelia did not ask the question aloud. Instead, she said, "Where's the creek?"

"Over there. We'll build our home there."

"Over there" was about a quarter mile from the stake. Now that they were so near, they all broke into a run. They came to a slight rise, then raced down a short slope. And there it was. Trees and shrubs grew on both banks. Water gurgled and tinkled over a stony bottom.

The three children rolled in the grass. They snatched handfuls of grass, and pelted one another. Finally they lay down on the bank, and drank of the cold clear water.

Cornelia's face came up, gasping, her chin and nose dripping. "Bernhard would have loved this," she said wistfully.

"But we wouldn't wish him back, would we?" said Father.

"N-no."

Then they were quiet, listening to the water.

"Hey! There they come!" shouted Anton suddenly. "There's the wagon."

On the level prairies it takes a long while, after you have sighted an oxcart, for it actually to arrive. But Peter Harms had no idea of waiting in idleness. He and the children gathered old sticks and dead branches. They broke the thinner ones into short lengths. They cleared a spot of grass, and started a fire. They fed it with thicker wood. When the wagon arrived, Mother jumped down quickly, carrying a kettleful of borscht that she had cooked the day before. She set it into the heart of the coals to reheat.

Then the whole family set to work to unload the goods that would be needed here. Some of it would go directly to Schoenfeld. The cookstove for one thing. But the airtight heater was to stay here. Till the snow came.

When the goods that were to stay had been unloaded the driver prepared to leave.

"He mustn't! He mustn't! Not without dinner!" exclaimed Grandmother.

"No, no, no. You stay," said Father, placing a hand on a horn of the nearest ox, and pointing to the fire, then to his mouth.

The man's face was dark—dark and secret. But a pleased look lit it for a moment. Then he was solemn and secret again. But he let Anton and Johann water the oxen. Then he tied them to a tree.

Mother and Grandmother's long skirts swished through the grasses as they unpacked the dishes and food. Grandmother dipped soup into an enamel bowl. "Here, Cornelia, this is for him." She had split two buns, and placed a piece of cold boiled sausage in each split. Silently Cornelia offered the food to the man.

The family sat down in a circle, including their silent guest. "Well, let us say thank you," said Father, and he took off his hat.

The wind rustled through the grass. The water chuckled as it tumbled over stones. A late meadowlark sang unexpectedly. Father's voice sounded warm and solemn as he thanked God for their new home, and that they could eat their very first meal here in company with a guest. He asked God to bless the stranger.

Cornelia glanced at the guest. He had been eating away before. But he sat for half a minute now, looking at them and yet *not* looking at them. It was a way that Indians and Metis had. Cornelia had noticed it before. Maybe they thought it bad manners to look directly at anyone Slowly he began chewing again. When he had finished his soup, he just sat holding the empty bowl.

"More?" said Cornelia. It was one word she had learned.

He let her take it and refill it. He must like the borscht. He ate that bowlful too.

As soon as the man had left, the work of settling in began. Father marked out the circle where the tent was to be. Mother and Grandmother took large butcher

107

knives and cut squares in the circle of grass. Then Father lifted the squares out with a spade, careful not to crumble them. The children carried them aside. The tent would be about 12 feet across when erected. It would be a crowded living space for six persons.

First the long poles had to be set up just so. The storeman had shown them how it must be done, and it looked simple. But it wasn't easy. When they were all in place, propping one another up, the skin had to be pulled down, all the way to the ground, and pegged into place. There was no centre post, and that was a good thing.

After the tent was up, Grandmother showed the children how to pile the sods closely around its base. This would help to shut out drafts. While they worked, Mother and Father arranged the boxes around the inner rim of the tent and set up the heater.

You could heat water on the stove top—or if you took off the lid you could sink the large fry-pan into the opening, over the coals.

Meanwhile the children had been dragging more dead branches out of the bushes. Suddenly a voice called, "Halloo!"

"An *Englaender!*" whispered Johann, nudging Cornelia.

Her tousled head popped around the edge of the tent. A horse and rider had come to a stop in front of the tent. The man saw the children and smiled.

"Are your folks at home?"

Folks? What was that? Home sounded like *Heim.* Cornelia darted to the tent front and ducked under the flap.

"Father, we have a visitor. He speaks only English."

He was a friendly man. He explained to father that he was a neighbor of theirs, and he wanted to see if there was anything he could do for them. The two men had a long talk. They liked each other.

"Have you ever farmed before?"

Father laughed, and shook his head. "I—am—a—*Lehrer*," he explained. "I—learn—children? Is that how you say?"

"A *teacher*?"

"Ja. Ja. I teach children."

"Where is the school?" He swung his arms at the empty prairies. "Where are your pupils?"

Pupils? Another strange word.

"Your students."

Ah, *Studenten*. "How you call them? *Pupils*?" said Father eagerly.

Their new neighbor laughed, and clapped Father's shoulder with his hand.

"You'll learn fast. You'll soon speak the queen's English with the best of us."

Father explained that the school was in Schoenfeld village. And the man wanted to know why they didn't move right in there.

"There—hole in ground. Dark. Not healthy," said Father, shaking his head. "Here—sun—*frische Luft* (fresh air)—" He waved his arms, and took long breaths of air.

"Fresh air! Right you are!" said the man. Then he added, "You teach me Deutsch, I teach you English." And they laughed together.

The man, whose name was Ronald Ross, entered the tent while Johann proudly held his horse. He shook hands with Mother and Grandmother. Grandmother had

109

tea ready in the Samovar. He had never seen a tea-making machine before. She gave him a glassful of tea and a piece of rock sugar to hold in his cheek while he drank it. He said the tea was very good.

Then he gave the boys each a ride over the prairies, in a great, wide loop. He dropped Anton last, waved at them all, and rode away. He was a very friendly man. Father thanked God at suppertime for such a good and helpful neighbor.

There was much work still to be done before night. At the Schanz shelters Grandmother had sewn large heavy sacks by hand. Everybody went out now to cut grass to stuff the sacks for mattresses. Of course they would have to be emptied again soon, or the grass would get mouldy and sour. It needed to be dried thoroughly. The boys put their sacks on boxes now. The rest spread theirs on the earthen floor. Cornelia's bed was a cosy one, as she slept with Grandmother. And Grandmother got the thickest feather tick to lay on the grass mattress, and the thickest feather comforter too.

Next morning all but Grandmother set out to walk to Schoenfeld. She said she meant to rest. It was a long, long time since she had been able to be alone.

"Always people, people around me. This aloneness—this I am going to enjoy for a change."

Mother teased her about wanting to do nothing. Grandmother admitted that she might do the wash. Thank the Lord, there was enough water here. And she would cook supper for them.

She stood in the tent door waving as they walked away. "Go—and come back safely."

Cornelia, Johann and Anton, running backward, waved too—until Cornelia stepped into a gopher hole, stumbled

110

against Johann, and all three fell in a laughing heap. Fortunately her ankle was not hurt.

"See? What did I tell you?" exclaimed Mother. She hadn't. But exclaiming "What did I tell you" was one of the Mother-habits they were used to. "Watch where you step."

Except for the smoke from chimneys, Schoenfeld didn't look like a village at all. But it was a busy place. Men, women, and children—all who were in the village— were at work. Some were still digging cellars. These were the latest arrivals. Some were cutting sods. All around the cellar homes you could see squares that were bare of grass. The squares of earth and roots and grass had been piled up around the cellar holes. A few tiny windows permitted a bit of light to enter the cellar homes. Not much. When the walls were piled up high enough, the men had laid poles across from end to end. The end walls were peaked. So the sods piled onto the poles sloped too. The sods used to cover the *simlins* were laid so as to overlap, to make the roof rain-proof.

Some of the *simlins* were finished. Their owners were away now, cutting grass for their cows and oxen. All the activity proclaimed, *Winter's coming, winter's coming. There's so little time, and so much to be done!*

The Harmses were invited to climb down steep ladders into this home and that one. A board partition usually separated the house part from the barn, and there were separate outside doors into the barn sections too. Instead of a ladder there would be a sloping bank of earth.

Cornelia could almost see what her mother was thinking. The cattle would be very close to the humans. How the cow smells would penetrate the clothes of the school children!

111

"It is for one winter only," she heard Father say reassuringly.

There was no scarcity of grass in this country, but this was the wrong season for making hay. However, as one of the men said to Father, it was the best they could do.

"I'm thinking we'll have a hard winter," he added.

The Harms family was anxious now to see their future home and the schoolhouse itself. They knew where to look for it, of course—right in the centre of Schoenfeld. It would serve as school, as Sunday meeting place and as their home, so the cellar was the largest one in the village. The walls were slightly higher, too. But the windows were just as tiny. There was a little sod entry, like a short tunnel. It was pretty low. Peter Harms could walk upright, but some of the men would have to stoop to enter. The stairway down into the cellar was steep and rough. And dark. You had to feel your way carefully.

Peter Harms pointed out to his family what an excellent thing it was that there was an entry. The winter's snows would not be able to block the stairwell.

In the dark *simlin* the Harmses peered around them, and their first impression was far from cheerful. They could not walk about freely, because their goods had been crowded together near the doorway. Beyond the heap of goods they saw desks that were nothing more than rough tables. There were backless benches, too, made of split logs, smoothed with axes. The walls were of earth below and sod above. The floor was of earth, and nothing more. One end of the area was partitioned off by rough boards. That part was to be the home for the teacher's family.

"No windows!" said Mother, and her voice trembled. "Not a single window."

112

SIMLIN USED BY THE EARLY
MENNONITE SETTLERS

Father sighed. "We'll have to use lamps. It's for one winter only."

When Mother was depressed, everyone was depressed. Cornelia, poking into dark corners here and there, had to think of the night of the thunderstorm in Schoenthal, in Russia—the night when her Mother hadn't made up her mind yet about the migration. Was she sorry now that she said yes? They had talked about Bernhard that night. The sea voyage was to make him better. But—it hadn't. Maybe their coming to Canada was a sad mistake.

Making the best of the situation now, Father and Mother decided where the stove was to be, and how they would arrange the boxes and crates and shelves.

"Come, children," called Father then. "Time to start for home."

Wordlessly they climbed the dark stairs and stepped out into the sunshine.

"Well! Teacher Harms!"

One of the Schoenfeld farmers was coming home with a load of half-cured hay. He stopped his team of oxen to shake hands all around. "God bless you in our midst!" he said heartily. "I hear you had Bible studies in your home in Russia. Are you planning to begin them here, too?"

"Yes, if there are those who wish to come."

"There will be. There will be. My wife was saying only this morning that she hoped you would continue the good work."

Father cheered up completely now. On the long walk back to their tent home, he spoke about his hopes. There would be opposition to the classes, he knew. One had to be prepared for that. Many Bergthaler people were suspicious of anything new, and home Bible study classes were considered very new.

Actually, they were as old as old can be! That was the way Menno Simons began his work 350 years before. At the very beginning of Mennonite history there was no way to spread his teaching except by private meetings in homes. Many people seemed to have forgotten that.

Or, perhaps they had never known it. They did things the way their parents and grandparents did them. They thought these were the right ways—the *only* right ways.

There were many things in this question that puzzled Cornelia. In school her father was supposed to use no readers *except* the Bible. But if a few grownups met on Sunday evening to study the Bible, their neighbors thought that was dangerous. How could it be?

Grandmother Siemens had supper waiting, true to her promise. A lot of clothes hung drying on tree branches and on surrounding brush. She had scrubbed—and boiled—all the wash that they were not wearing. Tomorrow, she said, they must wear clean things, and she would boil the rest. Tonight they better scrub their heads well. Maybe for once they would be rid of the tiny pests they had picked up on their long journey.

Grandmother asked about the Schoenfeld home, of course. She planned how they might make hanging shelves for storing food and other goods. She spoke so cheerfully as she served *Kielke* and fried onions, that Mother came out of her silent spell too.

The day ended with a general head scrubbing. And they went to bed in clean night shirts that smelled of sun and air. *Canadian* air, thought Cornelia sleepily.

VI
Friends and Neighbors

Cornelia could not tell what had awakened her. It wasn't the rain. The skins of the tent deadened the sound, so what one heard was more a swishing sound than a pattering of drops. And it wasn't the rest of the family, for everyone was still sleeping. But daylight had come, a grey sort of light. Cornelia could just glimpse the sky through the hole through which the poles stuck out.

Under her featherbed Cornelia dressed quickly and quietly. She was still barefooted when the sound came again, and now she knew this was what had roused her.

"Teacher Harms! Teacher Harms!"

"Father," she whispered, leaning over to touch his cheek. "Father!"

He snorted, jerked, then opened his eyes.

"There is somebody outside."

"Teacher Harms! Teacher Harms!" The muted call came again.

"You are dressed. See who it is," mumbled Father, still half asleep.

Carefully Cornelia stepped over Grandmother's feet, and poked her head partway through the tent flap.

"Who calls?"

"It is I, Daniel Martens."

Daniel Martens. Cornelia whipped her apron over her head and crawled out, bare feet and all. She and Daniel were looking unbelievingly at one another. He had grown much since spring, and anyway, he wasn't expected to come until 1876! What was Daniel Martens doing here in the rain outside their tent in Manitoba, Canada?

"How did you come so soon?" said Cornelia.

Daniel brushed her question aside. "How is Bernhard?" he asked eagerly.

Cornelia looked at him dully for a long moment. "You didn't hear? He—is—dead. He is buried over there, at Schanzenberg."

Abruptly he swung away. While she watched, he walked slowly toward the creek. He stood there, with his back toward the tent. His shoulders quivered. His hands went to his eyes, wiping his cheeks. And the rain kept falling.

"Who is it? Cornelia? Who is it?" called Father.

Shivering she crawled back into the tent.

"It is Daniel. Daniel Martens."

They brought him in out of the rain. When the whole family was up and dressed, and the bedding folded and stored for the day, they started a fire in the heater and Daniel could dry his clothes. Breakfast consisted of coffee and bread with lard. Nobody except Anton paid much attention to what they were eating this morning. They had to tell Bernhard's best friend about his death. There were minutes when no one ate or spoke. Everyone was crying quietly. They could hear the swish of rain, and the growling of the fire.

"I wanted to see Bernhard. I thought I *had* to see him. So the *Oberschulze* said I had better come with a group from the Molotschna colony. And I did. I did. I have a letter—" His damp coat had been hung up to dry. Daniel drew out a limp grey envelope.

"From Agatha!" said Mother. "Give."

"Isn't that Wilhelm's writing?"

"It's from both," said Mother, smiling in a particular way. "It has arrived. It has arrived!"

"Na, little Grandmother," said Father laughing at Mother. "Boy or girl?"

"A *baby*?" said Cornelia.

"A baby. A baby for Wilhelm and Agatha. A boy. And they have named him Bernhard Wilhelm. There is a note here—" Suddenly Mother's gay voice choked up.

"What does it say?" said Father gruffly.

"It says— it says— 'Bernhard, how will you like having a nephew named after you? We hope our Bernhard will be like his uncle'."

"They will soon hear now that Uncle Bernhard is with the Lord Jesus," said Grandmother Siemens softly.

They cheered up and asked Daniel all about his trip. He came across on the same ship that the Harmses travelled in—the "Laconia." "The sailors told us what dreadful storms you had," reported Daniel.

"Aha! Storms!" exclaimed Cornelia indignantly. "They told us that they weren't storms. They said we didn't know what a real storm was like. What we had was nothing but a heavy wind. *That's* what they said to *us*!"

"They were trying to fool us," said Anton.

"They were trying to calm our fears," said Father mildly. "Well, Daniel, what are your plans?"

He looked down. "I don't know. I don't have any."

"Are you thinking of going back to Martens?"

"No!"

"They have settled in Gruenfeld, I hear. That's only a few miles from here."

"No. The *Oberschulze* said I did not have to. He said a

big boy should get work in this country. He said in a few years I could have my own land! I am strong."

Father cleared his throat. "But meanwhile you are not big enough or wise enough to forget the necessary schooling. What about that?"

"I thought—the *Oberschulze* thought, if I could find a place in Schoenfeld, he would pay for the food and bed. That is what he said. He wrote it in a letter. And I thought I could maybe go to school with you yet this winter—"

He was going to miss Bernhard, though, thought Cornelia pityingly. They always were good friends, but Daniel was a rather slow student. Bernhard was his real teacher, and a very patient one. They helped each other. For when the school had an outing, Daniel helped Bernhard over the rough places. Sometimes he carried him on his back. That was the way it had been with them.

"We'll see —if we—can find—a place—for you—" said Father slowly.

"For this winter," remarked Mother, "there will hardly be a home in Schoenfeld that is not more crowded than ours."

That was as good as saying, "Perhaps he'd better live with us."

Teacher Harms looked at his wife, and she at him.

"He's a strong boy," added Grandmother.

"Would you like to stay with us?" Father still sounded hesitating.

Daniel needed no time to make up his mind. "If I only could!"

"Well, we'll think about it."

Cornelia hardly knew if she liked the idea. Did Daniel

119

think he was going to take Bernhard's place? He couldn't. Nobody could! But—he was strong. And he was good at farming jobs. In Russia he had had to work hard for his food and clothing. With Father in school so much of the time, and not a farmer in any case, maybe the Harmses did need a strong boy around to do the heavy jobs. It would be easier on Mother and Grandmother.

The rest of the day they wrote letters to Russia, and talked about little Bernhard. They tried the sound of their new titles. "Well, Uncle Anton, get me an armload of wood . . ." "Uncle Johann, an uncle ought to be able to write more neatly . . . ." Well, Aunt Cornelia, it's time to help prepare supper. How about peeling the potatoes?". . . . . ."Well, Grandfather Harms, may I ask you to move?"

"How can you be so heartless?" said Father, pretending to hobble with age.

In all their joking, no one said, "Uncle Daniel" this or that. Cornelia was glad of that.

But by the following evening the whole family was thankful that Daniel had arrived just when he did, and not a day later. He and Teacher Harms left early to walk to the Schanz shelters. Father hadn't forgotten his promise to dig a well there. The sheds were about empty now. But more and more immigrants would be coming next spring, and the well would be needed. The sun was out, and teacher and pupil set out, walking in wet, knee-high grass.

Cornelia, Anton, and Johann spent most of the forenoon tugging dead branches out of the bush, and breaking the thinner ones into short sticks. At eleven o'clock their neighbor Ronald Ross rode over. He brought them two gallons of milk and a dozen eggs!

"Ah, ah, ah! *Gut, gut!*" said Grandmother, beaming.

"You are *goot*," said the man, laughing. "But where is Peter Harms?"

They tried, all of them together, to explain where Father was, and what he was doing. It was hard to know if Herr Ross understood about the well. He seemed to understand about the Schanz shelters, because he rode away in that direction.

At noon Mother and Grandmother built a small fire outdoors, between stones. They set the long-handled frypan on the stones, and they made paperthin pancakes. They are best when eaten hot, so Grandmother handed them out to the three children in turn. Then she and Mother ate the next ones. With greasy lips and satisfied stomachs, the children played about on the grass, or beside the creek. They were all outside like that when they noticed the beat of horse hooves. A rider was coming fast, straight as an arrow.

"Could something be wrong?" said Mother anxiously.

"There are two riders," said Johann who had sharp eyes. "Two on one horse."

They were Ross and Daniel Martens. In spite of his ride, Daniel was pale as he slid to the ground. Ross wheeled his horse without even stopping, and took off for home.

"Something's happened!" said Mother.

"Accident," panted Daniel.

"Not killed!" shrieked Mother.

"No, no. But Teacher Harms has been hurt. Several ribs are broken, he thinks. Mr. Ross will bring him in a wagon—with horses. That is so much quicker than by oxcart."

"Thank God it is no worse," murmured Grandmother as she began to prepare a bed for Father.

The rest crowded round Daniel to hear what happened and how. Several men at Schanzenberg had begun digging two days ago. They went about eight feet down. Yesterday they had halted digging, because of the rain. This morning Teacher Harms and another man went down into the hole, and the walls began sliding in. The other man was hurt worse than Teacher Harms. Both of them might have been killed.

When Mr. Ross arrived with Father, the family heard the rest of the story. Ross tapped Daniel's shoulder. "Peter Harms . . . He would be dead but for this lad," he said.

Still not understanding the difficult English, they turned to where Father lay, breathing lightly on account of the pain in his chest. Father said it was true. If Daniel hadn't been on guard—he with his sharp eyes—they would most likely not have a father any more. Daniel first noticed the slideout. He warned them in time.

Daniel was red with pride and embarrassment.

Cornelia thought, What would it have been like if an oxcart had brought back the body of her father? This was what happened to two Mennonite families only a few weeks before. Two men got drowned. They were crossing the Red River in a canoe when it capsized. Their Indian rowers were dressed lightly. They got to shore safely. But it was a cold day, and the Mennonite farmers were wearing their heavy sheepskin coats. The coats dragged them down, and they didn't come up again. When the bodies were found, the son of one of the men had to drive the oxcart home. It took two slow sad days. He could not notify his mother. When the oxcart arrived she ran out eagerly to meet her husband—Cornelia turned off the thought with a shudder.

Dying . . . dying . . . dying . . . she thought drearily. Why must there be so much of it?

But Father was safe, even if he was in pain. The trip shook him up a lot. He groaned softly when Mr. Ross and Daniel carried him into the tent, and laid him down on his featherbed mattress.

"Oh, Peter, Peter," Cornelia heard her mother whisper. "What if you—"

"But I didn't die—I didn't die. God kept me safe." He smiled wanly at Daniel. "God sent the boy to us just in time."

Oh, but Daniel was a proud boy! And Grandmother mixed another bowlful of pancake batter, and she blew on the coals to start a quick hot fire again. But Father got only a cupful of hot milk and a small piece of toast. He refused even to try the pancakes. Anton and Johann thought they would have to be very sick indeed before they could say no to Grandmother's thin pancakes.

The very next day winter began. At noon snow began to fall. By nightfall, it came driving before a wind. The wind sighed around the tent, and went whimpering away through the nearby trees. It batted the smoke of the heater back into the tent, so they all sat there, red-eyed, and coughing. In a way it may have been a good thing. They helped to keep each other warm. But they knew too that they would have to move now. There could be no help for it. As soon as the wind died they must move. If only the tent wouldn't get buried first!

Peter Harms, who had had a poor night, insisted on sitting up in the morning, though both Mrs. Harms and Grandmother Siemens wanted him to lie still.

"Lying makes one weak," he said stubbornly. "I must be strong. Who would have thought winter would come so suddenly?"

The wind had died slightly, but snow still came sifting down. Father announced he planned to walk to Schoenfeld—

"Oh, but *never!*" gasped Mother.

"No, no, Peter," commanded Mother. "You stay here."

"I will go," said Daniel.

"Would you know the way? Ah, no. What if you got lost in the snow? I would not be able to forgive myself. It is my fault that we are here—"

"Whoa!" called a loud voice. "Halloo the tent!"

It was Ronald Ross, their *Englaender* neighbor. "Come to move your family to the village," he announced.

Many of his words were still strange, but he and Father managed to understand one another. The trip would not take very long. He had horses to draw the sleigh, not oxen. And the sleigh was a long open box. It had a lot of room.

Father went with the first load. But the moment he tried walking, he found out how weak he was. It was a good thing the sleigh was an open box, so a bed could be made for him.

"Peter will need you when you get there," said Grandmother to her daughter. "You go too. Cornelia can help me pack the rest of the things here."

They worked fast, though their fingers were stiff with cold now. The heater had to go with them, and it had to be cooled off in a hurry. They dumped the live coals in the snow, where they hissed and smouldered for a while.

"The snow is still falling," said Cornelia after a peek through the tent flap. "It's getting dark early." And she thought, What if Mr. Ross should lose his way? What if she and Grandmother would be left alone to freeze!

"Here, here, Cornelia. I need help. There is no time to waste. Quick, quick!" One could not be sad or lazy with Grandmother around. And almost before they were ready, Mr. Ross and Daniel had returned. Daniel told them that several Schoenfelder men had helped to carry Teacher Harms down the stairs. He had not had to walk. They had set up the cookstove too. The new home was almost ready now.

All four of them carried things to the sleigh. Their hands got icy. Their feet were sopping wet. They did not dare stop working. Night was coming fast. They had to be away from here soon.

"We'll leave the tent as it is tonight," said Mr. Ross.

They looked at him without understanding. He jabbed at the tent with his forefinger. "Tent—tomorrow morning," he said, talking very loudly.

"*Ja, ja. Morgen,*" (Yes, yes. Tomorrow) agreed Grandmother.

He laid one feathertick on a box for them to sit on, and tucked the second over and around them. Grandmother made Cornelia take off her wet shoes and stockings. She did the same. Under the tick she rubbed Cornelia's feet until some warmth came back.

But her teeth kept chattering as they drove into the snowy night.

At the Schoenfeld schoolhouse Mr. Ross stopped the team. (It still seemed very odd to find Canada was so upside-down, that horses would think Hoa meant Stop!) Ross jumped off the sleigh. Johann came running with a lantern. By its light Mr. Ross tossed back the top feathertick. He laughed to see four bare feet, one pair slender and small, the other decorated with corns.

"Stay here," he ordered Grandmother, and he put his hand on her arm and pressed down. Then he picked Cornelia up and carried her to the building. Through the little sod entry, (he had to stoop), and down the steep stairs. Into the cellar schoolhouse. Laughing he plunked her down on one of the rough tables, and ran out to bring Grandmother in. But he was too late. Barefoot as she was, she had come walking alone, carrying some food packages with her.

Supper was so late that night that everyone was almost too tired to eat at all. Mother had made tea in the Samovar. She cut some bread, and spread it with lard, and sprinkled it with salt. Everyone ate quickly. They had to decide about sleeping arrangements.

"Others will be sleeping on the earth this winter," remarked Grandmother. "And getting rheumatism. But we—we are the fortunate ones. We don't have to."

"Where else will we sleep than on the floor?" said Mother.

"On the school tables and benches, of course."

Father began laughing, which was bad for him. It made his chest hurt. But it seemed he couldn't stop laughing, for all that. "You are a real *Heldin* (heroine)" he told Grandmother. "Always stout of heart. And that idea of yours deserves a prize."

So that night—and all winter long—the school tables served as beds for Teacher Harms and his household. This meant folding and storing the bedding each morning, and bringing it out again each evening. It became Anton and Johann's job to roll and unroll the bedding as needed. It also meant that the whole family

126

had to stay up late, whenever there was a *Schulzenbott*. But these village meetings did not happen often.

Daniel proved a great help to the Harmses, especially now that Teacher Harms had to be careful of his strength. Daniel would carry tubfuls of snow in each morning. He and Grandmother had rolled an empty barrel up beside the kitchen stove. Daniel kept it full of snow water—and that's the finest soft water in all the world. When it was cold and clear, the taste was fine too. So they seldom bothered to run to the neighbors' well for water.

The couple that lived nextdoor was young, and their names were Abram and Huldah Thielmann. The lady reminded Cornelia a bit of Agatha. The Thielmann's lived in a *sarai*, not a *simlin*. It was an A-shaped roof set over a very shallow cellar. Inside it looked brighter than the other homes did. It was airier, and altogether more pleasant, thought Cornelia. The inside was covered with boards. The Thielmann's had pasted strips of paper over all the cracks to make it draftproof. The outside was thatched with bundles of grass. Huldah Thielmann had bound the bundles by hand, every one of them. But she wasn't as proud of that as of the fact that her Abram tied the bundles so neatly and closely in place on the roof. Next spring they hoped to build a permanent home, of course. But she was glad, she said, that her baby was not going to be born in a damp, dark cellar.

So the Thielmann's were going to have a baby too! Cornelia thought often of little Bernhard in Russia. It didn't seem fair or right that he was so far away. Little babies were so soft and cute and loveable. Imagine having one nextdoor!

Over many square miles the Mennonite settlers were

clustering in villages. Each village consisted of 20 or 30 households. Each had one main street, a half mile to a mile in length. Usually it cut straight through the middle of a section of land. On both sides of the street there were ten-acre squares marked out as farmsteads. Later they would plant trees and flowers and vegetables there. Later, too, they would build real houses. But this fall everyone was hurrying, hurrying to raise any kind of a shelter for the winter.

Teacher Harms was busy, too. His chest was sore still, but he could be up. School had begun, and each schoolday 35 boys and girls sat on the long rough benches at rough tables, learning to read and write, and do arithmetic. There were no blackboards, no maps, no pictures. There were hardly any books except the Bible. Beginners read the *Fibel*, the German primer. Ages 8 to 11 read in the New Testament. The older children read the Old Testament and studied the catechism.

The school *simlin* had been dark to begin with. Each snowstorm that winter clogged the windows completely. Often the pupils had to work by the light of two or three kerosene lamps.

It was a good thing that Teacher Harms was a good story teller. When the pupils got eyestrain from their work, he would tell them to put away their books, and listen. And they did. What stories he told! About Joseph, and Moses, and David. About Daniel. About Jesus. About Menno Simons, and missionaries like John Paton. He told them so vividly that the children would hardly have been surprised if one of the characters had walked into the *simlin*.

The children laid their heads on their folded arms on the tables. They gazed into the flames of the lamps—and they listened to Teacher's voice. It was like a magic trip into far countries.

The boys and girls all knew something about that. They too had come far, far. Sometimes they reminded one another of all the cities and countries they had glimpsed. They talked about Mr. Shantz, the Mennonite man from Ontario who helped the Mennonite immigrants to get settled here. All of the children had stayed for a while in the Schanz shelters. They talked about Mr. Hespeler, too. He was a government man, but he could speak German. And it was mainly through him that Canada had been opened to the Mennonites. He worked so hard for them that on his last visit to Russia that country expelled him! They were so angry that he had coaxed so many good farmers to leave that country for a new one.

Some of the children boasted they had actually seen Mr. Hespeler. And one day there was a knock on the schoolroom door. This alone was surprising. Mennonites did not believe in knocking on doors. But Teacher went to answer the knock—and in walked Mr. Hespeler! It was a great day for Schoenfeld school.

Their visitor looked mightily pleased. He said he had been worried. Suppose the immigrants—who had come here because *he* interested them in Manitoba—suppose they had come too late in fall? Suppose some of them had to stay out in the cold? He drove down from Winnipeg to see for himself. But all the busy people had worked hard, and everything seemed to be snug for winter. He told the boys and girls they had reason to be proud of their parents. He hoped they all would grow up to be hard working and thrifty and honourable as their parents were.

Mother invited Mr. Hespeler to stay for supper. She boiled a piece of ham for supper. (That showed how important the visitor was!) And she made some *pluma moos*, of dried prunes and apricots and apples. She had freshly baked bread too. It was a very special meal.

Cornelia remembered it long afterward. Not because of their visitor, though that was important. But because of what happened later that night.

Mr. Hespeler had hurried away right after supper. When he had left, Sarah Harms packed a basket with a piece of ham, and a bowl of *moos*, and some bread. She told Cornelia to run over to Mrs. Thielmann with the food.

"But it's so *cold* outside, Mother."

"It's only a short distance. Here, take, and go."

"But it's so *dark* outside."

"A big girl like you, afraid of the dark? Go."

So Cornelia went. She ran as fast as she dared with the *pluma moos* sitting there in the basket. In the dark she felt for the Thielmann door. Her teeth were chattering by the time she found the right spot and could lift the latch and walk in.

Mrs. Thielmann was hanging onto the doorframe, her eyes big. "Oh, Cornelia, Cornelia! Come in. Thank God you came!"

"Is—is anything wrong?"

"My man is away, and a storm is coming. And I think the baby is coming soon too."

"Should I call Mother?"

"Would you ask if she could come and stay with me? Will you do that? I'm afraid to stay alone. I was praying that I'd not have to stay alone!"

Would Cornelia? "Right away," she said.

130

SARAI USED BY SOME OF
THE EARLY SETTLERS

Running home, she hardly thought of the dark and the cold. She almost tumbled down the steep stairs in her hurry.

"Careful, careful," advised father.

"Where's Mother?" said Cornelia breathlessly.

"Aha!" said Father softly. "Is something important happening at our neighbors, perhaps?"

Cornelia smiled broadly. She ran past her father and into the dark kitchen. She whispered the exciting secret to her mother and grandmother.

"Of course I'll go," Mother washed her hands, tied on a clean apron, and got her coat out of the wardrobe which stood in one corner of the schoolroom. Grandmother had quickly collected some things for her to take with her. Mother picked up the bundle, and shouldered a big feathertick. Then she stood looking soberly at Cornelia. "Maybe I'll need help," she said. "Would you want to come with me?"

Cornelia felt afraid—but excited too. Together they went out into the night, which was turning stormy. They carried a lantern, and in its tiny light-circle you could see white flakes streaking past. Both of them were puffing and breathless by the time they reached the Thielmann *sarai*.

Huldah Thielmann hugged both of them. A moment ago her eyes had been big with fright. But now she had friends around her.

"How cold it is in here!" exclaimed Sarah Harms when she had taken off her coat.

"Keep your overshoes on," advised their hostess. "This place is very drafty."

"Drafts! Is that what you call it? More like a wind, it seems to me." And Sarah Harms began adding more

132

wood to the fire. It was a good thing Abram Thielmann had carried in a lot of wood. It was stacked waist high along one wall of the *sarai*.

"Where is your man?" Cornelia thought her mother sounded a bit impatient.

Huldah Thielmann must have noticed it too. "He had to go to Winnipeg. Don't blame him. He had to go. Ah, you don't think he'll be lost in this storm do you?"

"No, no. No, no," said Mother comfortingly. "Don't be afraid. We are in the hands of God. He will take care of you."

But the wind blew more and more fiercely, and the *sarai* grew colder and colder. The lamplight often flickered on account of the draft. Cornelia found out why her mother had brought the feathertick along. It was to be Cornelia's bed. She spread half on the bearskin rug on the floor, and told Cornelia to take off her overshoes and shoes, lie down, and use the other half as cover.

Cornelia had been shivering so hard that her teeth rattled. Gradually she breathed her own warmth into the feather bed and the shivering lessened. She watched her mother put a wash boiler onto the stove, and fill it with snowwater from a drum near the door. She was just drifting, drifting off to sleep when she sat up with a terrified jerk. She and Mother looked wildly at one another. Someone was shooting. There— Another shot! And another!

"The Indians! The Indians!" Cornelia wanted to scream the words, but only a squeak came out.

And now she saw that Huldah Thielmann was shaking all over too—but she was laughing. She laughed so hard the tears streamed down her cheeks. *Laughing*. What was the matter with her? There went another shot. And another!

133

"It's n-nothing," gasped Mrs. Thielmann. A shaky finger pointed up at the A-shaped ceiling. "It's the paper. The boards were green. From the indoor heat they have dried—."

"And they have shrunk," finished Mother with a sheepish grin. "Ah, I see. And in shrinking they crack the paper. And that sounds like a gunshot."

The two women laughed comfortably together, but Cornelia felt embarrassed as she sank back into her nest. It was a good thing that Johann and Anton weren't here. Or Daniel. If there was one thing Cornelia didn't like it was giving the boys an excuse to laugh at her folly. (Yet she had never minded much when Bernhard teased her. He was a tease too.) She hoped Mother . . . wouldn't . . . . tell . . . . .

That was Cornelia's last conscious thought until she came awake suddenly. What had awakened her? Where was she? How cold it was here—wherever here was. She had stuck her head and shoulders out of the feather tick, but she drew back quickly again. There— That was the sound. A thin mewling bleat . . . Then came an angry bawl.

"Shhhh . . . . shhhhhh . . . ."

The *baby!* Eagerly Cornelia's eyes roved around the *sarai*. The lamp beside Mrs. Thielmann's bed was turned down low. Mother had taken the lid off the stove top. The coals in the stove cast a red glow over her face. She was holding a bundle in her arms, shushing it, singing to it very, very softly.

"Mother," said Cornelia in a whisper.

"Ah, are you awake?" Mother turned the wick a trifle higher.

"What time is it?"

"Shhhhh . . . Mrs. Thielmann's sleeping. We've been very busy, I can tell you. It's four o'clock."

"Is the storm still blowing?"

"Listen!"

Cornelia pushed the feather tick away from her ear. It was still blowing.

"I'd pity any one who has to be out in that," said Mother.

"And the baby?"

She laughed softly. "She has come. Should I put her in with you while I get a bed ready for her?"

"Oh, yes. yes!"

Only a crumpled red face could be seen. Cornelia raised on her elbow to examine the face by the faint light. She touched it with the back of a cautious finger. So fat—and so soft—and so tiny!

Mother had pulled the lower drawer out from a chest of drawers. It was filled with baby things—grey flannel diapers, and striped flannel dresses and bibs. Mother stacked them on a box that was ordinarily used as a chair. She warmed a feather pillow over the stove, and placed it in the drawer. Then she lifted the baby out of Cornelia's reluctant arms.

"Couldn't I keep her here?"

"Shhhh . . . . Too close to the floor," whispered Mother. "It's cold down there."

So the new baby went to bed in a drawer on top of the kitchen table.

"Now you go back to sleep." Mother was just going to turn the wick of the lamp down when there was a stumbling sound at the door. It swung open suddenly. Icy air and a swirl of snow came in, but not alone. A man stood there, gasping and swaying.

"God be thanked—God be thanked—for the light in the window. I—I—" He almost fell, but Sarah Harms who had kicked the door shut, got her shoulder under his to steady him.

"Cornelia!" she called softly but urgently.

Huldah had heard. "What's wrong?"

"Nothing. Nothing. God has brought your man safely back home. That is all."

"Is that so? Are you there, Abram?"

He still couldn't talk. Mother had him propped in a chair before the fire now. "Come, Cornelia, stand here," she commanded. She hurried to the bed in the corner and spoke soothingly to Mrs. Thielmann. "You lie down. He's all right. He's been out in the dark and cold, but he'll soon be able to talk to you."

At that moment the baby began crying. "Ahn—ahn—ahn—ahn—" Mother ran to the drawer. She scooped up the little bundle.

"What—is—it?" mumbled Abram Thielmann.

"A girl. Here, Cornelia. Get into bed and I'll give her to you—since you're awake anyway. We'll leave just a tiny hole for air. Cover her face."

So Cornelia got to hold the baby again. She rocked her, shushing her, patting her back. And the baby went to sleep.

Mother who was helping Thielmann out of his frozen mitts and cap and overshoes, smiled across at Cornelia. "I'll make some hot coffee," she said. "That will warm you up inside."

"May I—see Huldah?"

"No, no. Not yet. You stay away from her! You are much too cold for her. You need something to eat."

She found some soup to reheat. His fingers were so

136

stiff and shaky he couldn't hold the spoon, so she poured the soup into a cup.

"Drink that. All of it."

Obediently he did. But his fingers hurt badly by now. He set down the cup. He waved his hands about. He wrung them. He drew in his breath with a hissing sound. His cheeks must have been frozen too. They hurt. He sipped soup and hissed by turns. He was rocking with pain and beating his stockinged feet on the plank floor. But he did it all quietly, because his wife had drifted off to sleep again.

"I thought I'd never see home again," he said through swollen lips. "I wondered what would happen to Huldah and the baby—if I froze to death. But God has been good to us."

"He is a very present help in time of trouble," agreed Mother.

Cornelia, drifting off to sleep again, felt the little bundle lifted out of her arms. The next thing she knew it was morning. The storm had died. The sun was out.

Cornelia and her mother went home without breakfast. She hated to tear herself away from the baby—but she had a lot of news to tell!

VII
First Canadian Winter

Every quiet day after that blizzardy night, Cornelia could be seen running to the Thielmanns for an hour or so. In spite of the cold *sarai*, the baby grew and throve. She was named Sarah-Cornelia, after her first two nurses! Her father called her Suschki—Little Sarah. Or his Kruschki—little apple. But her mother mostly called her Nellie. Little Nellie was one bright spot that winter.

It was a hard winter, long and cold and difficult. Most of the settlers had too little food to last through the winter and too little money to buy more. Then leading men of the villages got together, and decided to try to borrow some money for the purchase of food. They made a $20,000 loan from the Mennonites who lived in Ontario. These were established Canadians, not new settlers. And because they were fellow Mennonites, they were interested in the newcomers. The money was used to order a shipment of dry beans and bags of flour. This was to come by way of the Great Lakes, Huron and Superior, then down the Red River. The barge got as far as Emerson on the Manitoba border. There it froze fast in ice.

This meant that the new settlers had to go by oxcart to bring the goods home. And early as it was in the season, the temperature dropped suddenly to more than forty below zero. At Emerson no stable room could be found for the oxen. Their lips and noses were badly frozen, and for weeks they had difficulty nosing out their feed. But the lives of many settlers were saved.

Peter Harms had thought he had bought enough flour for his family to last the winter. They were six persons now, though. And when there's little to eat except food made of flour, one sackful disappears fast. They were grateful for their share of the imported flour and beans.

Each village bought a few old cows from their Indian neighbors. Schoenfeld held a butchering bee at the school one Saturday. Several men came together to slaughter the cows and divide the meat fairly, according to the size of the households. The schoolroom tables were piled with heaps of meat and soupbones that day. When the last heap had gone, Sarah Harms and her mother scrubbed the tables and benches free of tallow. They tidied up the earthen floor too. Tomorrow was Sunday. Today's butchershop had to be ready to be tomorrow's house of worship. And what a pity it would be if their Sunday blacks would get spotted with tallow!

When the tables were dry Johann and Anton began their nightly chore. They placed the tables together, two by two. They spread out the hay-stuffed mattresses, and the featherticks and comforters. Father had laid two boards across the rafters of the *simlin*. This was the daytime storage space for the bedding. Each morning the boys tossed it up. Each evening they hauled it down. Usually there was much noisy laughter from the boys. When Father shushed them they explained that you had to laugh—or get angry. The feather ticks were so awkward to handle. Not heavy, but bulky and *obstinate*.

Thin curtains partitioned off the corner where Grandmother and Cornelia slept. Snug in bed this Saturday night, Cornelia thought of yesterday's school time.

139

Tuesdays and Thursdays you studied maps and numbers. On Monday, Wednesday and Friday you studied reading, spelling, and Bible stories. Friday afternoons were special. Father always tried to make them interesting. The pupils practised good writing. They drew pictures. They recited poems. They listened to adventure stories told by Teacher Harms.

Daniel loved the adventure stories as much as anyone. But he didn't care for memorizing poetry, though he liked to listen to it well enough. He drew the best pictures in school. He always had. But he hated good-writing practise. All the pupils were expected to shape the letters exactly the way Teacher Harms did. Daniel said he *couldn't*. Father said it was only that he *wouldn't*. He said that anyone who could draw as well as Daniel, ought to be able to write well.

This day Daniel got into trouble with Teacher Harms. Not serious trouble. He did not get a whipping. But Teacher Harms spoke seriously to him about setting a bad example. He, the biggest boy there.

Daniel's lower lip trembled. He said he knew he was the biggest boy there—and the oldest and strongest. What he wanted to do was to quit school right then and there!

Cornelia knew her father was more shocked and disappointed than angry. At the supper table Daniel looked downcast but determined. He hardly ate anything. When they left the table, Father told him with a sigh that he could have his wish. Leave school—go to work—if that was what he wished!

"Monday?" said Daniel, brightening up.

"If that is what you want," said Father again.

"And—and—" The boy rubbed his ears, his forehead.

140

"—could I still live with you, Teacher Harms?"

"Of course. This alters nothing of our former arrangement."

Daniel swung around quickly so his back was turned. Cornelia saw his eyes glitter. He was crying—great big boy! It reminded her of the day when he heard that Bernhard was dead. He went quickly now to get the tub to carry snow in for melting. Then he split wood and helped the younger boys carry that into the kitchen.

And this morning, Saturday, he announced that he intended to go into the woods this winter. Abram Thielmann had offered him a job, chopping down trees and squaring logs. In spring they would be ready for building the Thielmann home.

Cornelia was trotting home from a visit with Huldah Thielmann and little Susch, when she bumped into Daniel. She was facing into the wind, a cold wind. She had been hanging her head to shield her forehead, which is why she did not see the boy. She bumped into him so hard that her feet slipped out from under her. But she scorned his help in getting to her feet again.

"You did that on purpose!" she flashed out at him.

"What?"

"Stand in the path, so I had to bump into you! Isn't there enough room on the side for standing? The path is for walking."

"Ach, Cornelia, don't be so angry," he pleaded. "I wanted to ask you something."

"Well, be quick. I am cold. Br-r-r-r-r!"

"Is he—is your father angry with me? For quitting school?"

"He is disappointed," she said severely. "Very disappointed."

Daniel looked so miserable that she began to repent her severity, and she quite forgot the stinging wind.

"I—I just couldn't stand it. It wasn't the learning, so much. I will never make a scholar, but I could learn something. But I couldn't *stand* it. In school—with Teacher Harms—but no Bernhard." His chin was jumping.

So that was it. Cornelia, trotting on again, felt frozen tears rolling down her own cheeks.

"What is wrong?" exclaimed Mother the moment she saw Cornelia's face. "Is Mrs. Thielmann sick? Or the baby?"

"No, no." A smile flashed across Cornelia's face. Little Kruschki was getting cuter every day. But Mother still wanted to know the reason for Cornelia's tears, and Father happened to be standing by. After a bit of prodding she told them what Daniel had just told her.

"Ah," said Teacher Harms, "So that's it. He is a big boy, almost the size of a man. But he has the faithful, tender heart of a small boy. Maybe it is best he works off some of his grief by hard work in the forest.

Many fathers and big brothers were out in the woods now. When Monday came the Harmses saw Daniel off. Mother had baked *Schnettke* for him to take along. Some of them were folded, with a bit of brown sugar in the folds. Daniel looked proud and important as he and Abram Thielmann rode away behind the patient oxen. It was 50 miles to the forest. They would be gone several weeks at a stretch.

"Visit my Huldah and Little Susch often," Thielmann called over his shoulder."

"We will, we will!"

"If only the oxen don't freeze their noses again,"

142

remarked a bystander. "Never, never in Russia have we had such a cold."

It was a hard winter, especially for the cattle. Many died off fast. Those especially that were sheltered in *sarais* instead of *simlins*. The wind fairly whistled through the cracks. But those with warmer stables had their troubles, too. They suffered longer. About the only feed they got was the half-cured slough hay, and it had little food value. Before long the settlers found that their cattle were too weak to get to their feet in the mornings. Yet they must get' up if they were to live. So each morning the men and the boys of the village went from barn to barn. With ropes and slings they lifted the weak animals to their feet—and they wondered how many would live till spring.

The winter seemed to drag on and on.

In school things went on much as usual. The children grew listless and tired, but no one was starving. Pupils brought their slates to school, and a bottle of water and a rag with which to clean their slates. The blackboard, which was nothing but a board painted black, needed a washing with soap and water after each use. The school had two maps—actually two! One showed the western half of the earth ball, the other showed the eastern half. One of the first things Teacher Harms had the older pupils do was to trace the journey they had come, from Bergthal colony, Russia, to Manitoba, Canada. Ten thousand miles. Eleven trains . . . . five ships . . . two wagons. For the journey that began with a wagon trip also ended with one for most of them.

And for what had they come? Sometimes Cornelia could not help wondering. *For what had they come?* Day after day they ate the same food. *Prips* and bread for breakfast. Bread and *prips* for dinner. *Prips* and bread for supper. Day after day after day. It could be worse. If that shipment of flour had not come there would be no bread at all.

Prips was the common coffee substitute. Some made it of wheat, some of barley, some of a mixture of rye and barley and wheat. (Each household had the very *best* recipe, of course.) You bought the grain. You washed it well, making sure to pick out all the pebbles, and every bit of wild buckwheat. After that you dried the grain. Then you roasted it slowly in the oven until it turned a deep brown. The smoke of it stung your eyes.

It became Anton's daily chore to pour roasted grain into the cup of the coffee-mill and grind it fine. First thing in the morning the pot of *prips* went onto the stove. As soon as Father had built the morning fire. It sat there all day long, at a low boil. The whole *simlin* smelled of *prips*, day and night.

Once in a long while the family would have a cupful of cream given to them. *Prips* with cream was delicious. But fewer and fewer families had any milk or cream for their own use, let alone to share with others.

Any change in the daily routine was a big event.

One day Cornelia heard a bumping, thumping sound at the door. She ran to open it. Before her stood a little man, with a pack on his back. His face was bearded, and icicles hung around his mouth and chin. Hoarfrost had gummed up his eyebrows and lashes. He slid his pack off his back and onto one of the school tables. He was puffing and blowing, but he smiled too.

The boys, catching sight of him, shouted, "A pedlar! a Jewish pedlar!" Which wasn't very polite, and Mother was embarrassed for them. But this was like being back

144

home in Russia. Jewish pedlars came frequently to the Bergthal colony.

This one didn't act offended a particle. He nodded, chuckling. "*Ja, ja. Ich will mache ei' Geschaeft!*" he said. (I want to do business.)

Cornelia felt a lump in her throat. This was *exactly* as in Russia. She hadn't known she was so lonesome for home.

The pedlar had much the same items for sale too. And he liked bargaining.

Teacher Harms had never enjoyed it. One of the things he liked so much about Canada was that the store owners set the price, and you either bought a thing or you didn't buy it. He thought bargaining a great waste of time and a nuisance. But Grandmother enjoyed it, and she hadn't had a chance in many months. She welcomed the pedlar joyously.

"How much is that grey print?" she asked.

"Twelve cents a yard." He flicked open the bolt of cloth. "See there. Pretty, isn't it? And only twelve cents. Feel the quality."

"Quality!" she sniffed. "I shouldn't wonder if it was full of stiffening. Come, I'll give you three cents a yard. It isn't worth that."

"Three cents!" The trader clutched his hair, pulled his beard, and groaned. "Three cents, she says!" The icicles had fallen from his hairy face by now. You could hear them crunching under his feet as he jogged up and down to show how unfair Grandmother was. "A grandmother and a mother, and she says three cents! For this beautiful, beautiful cloth!"

Grandmother looked disdainful. "Come down, come down. It isn't worth twelve cents, I tell you."

145

He shook his head mournfully. "I will be taking the bread and butter from the mouths of my children, but because you are so good—a mother and a grandmother—I will let you have it for eight cents."

"Four," said Grandmother promptly.

He sighed. "If it must be, it must. I'll let you have it for six. But that is positively my last offer."

"Keep it, keep it. I don't think I'll be needing the print after all," said Grandmother, who was enjoying herself immensely.

"How much will you give me?" said the pedlar, sounding depressed.

"Five." And that is positively *my* last offer."

She got it for five. And both she and the pedlar were pleased. She had him cut off ten yards, and watched to make sure he was not cheating on the amount.

Cornelia wasn't interested in the grey print. Guinea hen gray. The shawls were much prettier. They were 30 inch squares, black, and covered with embroidery. She thought of her plain black Sunday dress, the one she had worn to Agatha's wedding. It would be lovely to brighten it up with a flowered head scarf. But the pedlar's price was a dollar and fifty cents. As much as a man could earn in three days! And even if he went down to 75 cents, that still would be as much money as would buy fifteen yards of print. Money was too scarce for that.

There were combs in the pack, wooden ones, rubber ones. The rubber combs did not tug your hair so mercilessly as the wooden ones did. But—the family comb still had only two teeth missing. It clearly wasn't time to buy a new one.

Grandmother bargained for and bought some needles and thread, and some ribbon. It was supper time then, and Mother asked the pedlar, Aaron Joldstein, to stay and share their meal. It consisted, of course, of bread and *prips*, with just a bit of brown sugar strewn over the bread.

They were about to begin eating when there was a knock on the door again. A stranger must be at the door. Cornelia ran to open it.

"Well, hello," said the visitor. It was Ronald Ross.

"Thought I had to come and see how you folks were doing," he said to the family.

Everybody brightened up at the sound of his voice. They had not seen Mr. Ross in a good while, but they knew he was their friend. How had they been? he wanted to know. Was Teacher Harms well over his chest injuries? Where was the big boy who helped with the moving job? Out in the woods, eh? Were they all well? And why was Cornelia getting prettier every day? and how about offering him some of that good bread?

"Will he really want to eat with us?" asked Mother timidly when Father translated his last sentence.

He seemed to understand what she said. "Just try me," he answered. And he sat down on the bench beside Johann, facing Cornelia.

"Let us pray," said Father in English, folding his hands, and bowing his head.

He'll laugh, thought Cornelia. She didn't think *Englaender* people thanked God for food. Maybe they didn't pray to God at all! But Mr. Ross's face was as pleasant as usual when he held his cup for Grandmother to fill it with hot *prips* a moment later. Mother sliced more bread. Father strewed sugar thinly for the boys. Mr. Ross ate his bread without sugar, but he asked for a second cupful of *prips*. And he praised Mother for the quality of her bread.

147

But after supper came the interesting part. He stayed to talk with Father. Teacher Harms had bought some English books, a dictionary and a grammar among them. He had studied a bit every evening, and he could speak the language much better than in fall. He understood Ronald Ross better, too. Though supper was done, the whole household still clustered around the school table where the lamp sat. Grandmother had her knitting out. Mother was patching a pair of pants. Cornelia was darning a pair of woolen stockings. She was considered old enough now to keep her own things in order.

Their neighbor wanted to know about Mennonites. Where they came from, why they moved about so much, and why they lived in villages.

"In Russia it was necessary," said Father. "For protection from robbers. And it was good in many ways. So we could have our own schools. So we could help each other. So we could visit without having to drive much. There were many reasons."

"But here! You don't need to cluster together. There is room to spread. Why don't you spread?"

Father asked a question in his turn. "Is it your thought that the village system won't work here?"

Teacher Harms had trouble with the English "th" and "v" and "w" so he actually said "taught" for "thought", and "fillage" for "village", and "von't vork" for "won't work." He had asked his guest to be sure to correct his pronunciation, so he did. Cornelia and her brothers practised saying "village, village, village . . . won't work, won't work, won't work, won't work" while the guest nodded and laughed. Then he grew sober again.

He asked especially about the *Streifenfluren*, the long strips of land into which the village farmers cut their

148

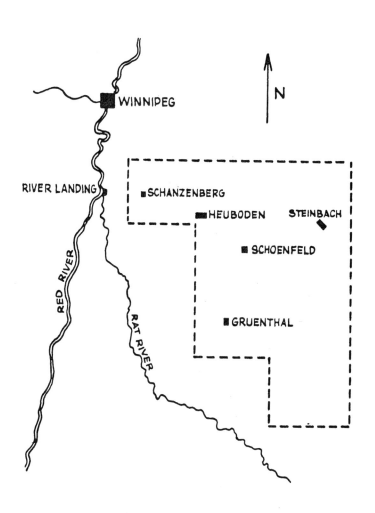

EAST RESERVE, WITH SOME OF THE
FIRST MENNONITE SETTLEMENTS
IN MANITOBA, 1874

land. Some might be a mile in length, some a half mile or even less. The land would be divided fairly, so that every farm had the same acreage.

Father drew the plan of a typical village. He showed how the strips were numbered so each farmer had to travel the same distance from piece to piece to piece. All alike, all fair.

"But, man, how can you?" burst out Mr. Ross. "The areas are so different. I mean, the land differs from quarter to quarter. You'll find swampy spots, and good open grasslands, and forest—all mixed. I tell you, it can't be done. Dividing it fairly, I mean. It won't work."

"It worked in Russia."

"What kind of land did your people farm there?"

"The steppes. They had never been successfully farmed before. Our people proved that it was good for farming. It has been so always. Where our people have went—have gone—they have transformed the area."

Mr. Ross drummed his fingers on the table and looked thoughtful. "Well, maybe," he said.

"Look, my friend," said Father. "See the advantages—advantages—of living in fillages. If we lived far apart, could we have a school this winter?"

"No. You have a point there."

"Could we help ourselfs when there is sickness and dying? Now we know we are never alone, never far from help. Many of us do not have oxen or horses for driving. What if my family sat now, lonely and alone, on a piece of land, months and months—and in this Canadian cold. Our spirits would droop and freeze as much as our bodies. So I say again, Could we help one another so easily? Could we borrow axes and hammers and saws from each other?"

"Is that what is happening now?"

Father nodded. "Some are too poor to buy their own. So they borrow. They borrow for a few hours from this farmer, and for a few hours from another. Never all day from the same one. All is fairly ordered."

"Who orders it?"

"The *Schulzenbott*."

"That's like a town council, is it?"

"It is like it—and it is not like it. It is part of the village structure. It is part of our church life. The church and the village are one."

Mr. Ross rubbed his bristly chin. "If you are so much in favor of the system, why did you not join the village? Why did you choose to homestead apart like that?"

"I am not a farmer," said Father meekly. "What if I fail? Then the whole village would suffer. My debt becomes everybody's debt. This way, my failure is mine alone."

"How do you plan to farm at all?" Their guest was full of blunt questions.

"Part of my pay as teacher," explained Father, "will be that each farmer in the village, each father who has children in school, will plow and seed one acre for me in spring."

"There you go again," said Mr. Ross, rumpling his hair. "Twelve farmers, twelve span of oxen, twelve ploughs all travelling across the prairies to plough one acre apiece for you. Man, what waste of *movement!*"

Father was laughing now. "Not twelve. Count twenty. There are twenty farmers whose children I am teaching this winter. The school lasts for half the year only. So half a year I am a farmer—if I can learn—and half a year a teacher. And—" He smiled slyly at Mr. Ross—"with

151

such a wise neighbor as you, I should learn much of the new ways."

Mr. Ross laughed, and rose to go. Out of one bulging pocket he drew a package. It contained a pound of butter.

"From my wife. Sorry I forgot about it. A bit soft now, I'm afraid."

"Ah, butter!" Mother was so pleased, she lost her shyness over speaking in a new language. "Too bad you not bring out before. Then you would not have to eat the bread that is so dry."

"Mrs. Harms, I have never enjoyed a supper more in my life than your fine bread and your—how do you call the drink?"

"*Prips*," said Cornelia, Johann and Anton in chorus.

He tried the sound, but now it was their turn to become language teachers.

"You must make a little r-r-r-r-r when you say it," they told him.

"Pr-r-r-r-ips!" he said. The door was closing behind him, but he stuck his head back in again.

"One thing more, Peter, about your Str-r-r-reifen-flur-r-r-ren." He was teasing the children, and they knew it. But he was serious too. "What happens to all the strips of grass between the Str-r-r-reifen? Waste. Pure waste! That's not economical farming, man!" He raised his hand, said goodnight, and was gone.

Father looked seriously at the door through which his neighbor had just disappeared. "That man is worth listening to, I think," he said. "What, Friend Goldstein are you going too?"

For the pedlar, who had been silent most of the evening, dozing in a corner, had his pack strapped to his back again.

152

"Yes. Yes. Time for me. Well, Mother, goodbye. You will not be sorry for your purchases. But my poor children! My poor children! They will have to starve now."

"Ach, yes," said Grandmother laughing. "Our hearts bleed for them."

"Will they really have to starve?" said Anton anxiously when the door had closed behind the pedlar. "And why did he call you mother? He's not my uncle, is he?"

Everybody burst out laughing, and Anton hung his head with embarrassment.

"No, no. No, no," said Grandmother. "We Mennonites are good bargainers, but the descendants of Abraham can still outbargain us."

"But he *called* you mother!"

"He says that to every old woman."

Mother said wistfully, "I could almost imagine myself back in Russia. It seems homelike to have a pedlar drop in like this."

"I hope he does not drop in too often," said Father humorously. "We do not have many fifty cents to spare."

Letters had come that day. Letters from relatives in the United States. The weather in Kansas wasn't nearly as cold as in Canada. There were several letters from Russia too. One from Aunt Gerda, another from Agatha and Wilhelm.

Sarah Harms was plain lonesome tonight. While washing dishes she sang softly, *"Nach der Heimat moecht ich ziehen, nach dem teuren Vaterhaus . . ."* (To my home I would like to go, to my Father's home) It had a sad melody, sad enough to make anyone want to cry. And Christmas time was almost here. That is the time of year when you most want to be at home. But—where was home now?

Not in Schoenthal, Bergthal colony, Russia. Strangers were living in many of the homes now. The Harms family could never go back. Never. And Bernhard would not be there even if they could return.

Cornelia, snuggling down between her feather ticks, heard her parents still talking in low voices about the letters.

"But we chose Canada because our young men had no assurance they would not have to fight if we went to the United States."

"They won't have to fight. Cousin Maria said the government man told them so. He said the United States will never, never fight. Never again."

"Sarah, are you sorry you said yes?"

There was a long, long silence. Then Mother sighed. "If I answer according to my feeling I would say yes—Yes, I *am* sorry. But that is not right. I know it is not right. We came to Canada because we believed God wanted us to. And God does not change His mind." Then she added, "Pray for me, Peter. Pray that I may do God's will gladly."

Of all seasons, thought Cornelia, Christmas should be a very happy one. In school each pupil was learning a Christmas *Wunsch* (verse.) And on the last day of school, in the afternoon, they sang Christmas songs, and each child recited his *Wunsch*. Then Teacher Harms said a few words about the coming of the Lord Jesus into this world. He wished them a *Froehliche Weihnachten* (Merry Christmas). And he gave each child a card with a pretty bird and a Bible verse on it. The school sang "*O du Froeliche Weihnachtszeit*" (O thou joyful Christmas time!) and the school was dismissed. It would not open again until after New Year's Day.

Christmas church services lasted through three mornings. And because Christmas was so important, most of the children in Schoenfeld came with their parents. Usually, on Sundays, children under twelve stayed at home. Teacher Harms did not agree with this custom. In his family every child went to church every Sunday, but many people thought this peculiar. And it had been a lonesome thing for Cornelia to sit through the services when there was no other girl of her age there. Now she was thirteen, almost, so other girls of her age came too quite regularly.

For Christmas Father opened the barrel in which the whole pig was pickled. For Christmas dinner they had *pluma moos*, and cold sliced ham, and buns, and peppernuts. Father looked mysterious at the table. They knew he had planned a surprise. Later he brought out a small sackful of sunflower seeds. Nobody had known he had brought them all the way from Russia for this purpose. He kept some for spring seeding, but Mother roasted the rest in the oven. The aroma filled the *simlin*. Somehow it made the season more festive.

And next came New Year's celebration. All through the settlement people had been saving raisins and lard and eggs. On the last day of the old year mothers made New Year's cookies. They were light balls of yeast-dough that were cooked in hot fat. The spoonfuls plopped down. They sank out of sight, then bobbed up, sizzling. Mother's fork came down and flipped them over, so both sides were cooked an even brown. The delicious smell lingered in the *simlin* for a long while. It made one hungry all day long.

Daniel Martens had come home for Christmas. Of course, he was home for every possible weekend too, but during the Christmas holidays Mr. Thielmann stayed with his family and never went to the forest at all. So Daniel was free too.

He enjoyed life in the woods. Many men and boys worked together there. They joked a lot, and played pranks on one another. They had built a *sarai* for the oxen, and another for the men. Instead of thatching, they used spruce boughs to cover the roof. Daniel said their *sarai* certainly was cosier than the Thielmann's. That was because they were in the heart of the woods, where wind rarely could be felt.

He told stories of how he tamed a bluejay to eat crumbs out of his hand. He told of seeing animal and bird tracks. Anton and Johann crowded around him each time he came home, eager to hear more about life in the woods.

Everyone was busy getting ready to build a permanent home. Everybody except the Harmses. While other fathers used axe and saw in the woods, Teacher Harms sat in the schoolroom. Sometimes Cornelia worried about that. Of course, when spring came they would move back into their tent again. But for the *whole summer*? Living like Indians was fun for a while, but would one want to do it all the time?

Cornelia never mentioned her worries on the subject. It might make Mother feel worse. This winter was hard on her.

It was hard on everyone. Beside the cattle that grew weaker day by day and finally died, more and more people died too—old people and babies especially. Funeral after funeral was held in the schoolhouse *simlin*.

156

Sometimes Cornelia felt she could hardly bear it. Usually she ran away for a visit with Little Suschki. But even the baby wasn't gaining weight as she ought to.

Spring came slowly at last. The snow began melting. Settlers coaxed the remaining cattle up the earthen ramps and into the weak sunshine. There they stood, soaking up the feeble warmth. Their coats were rough. Their eyes looked sunken and sad. But gradually they began licking at the spears of grass that were coming up. Spring had actually arrived. A new life cycle had begun.

On the yards of Schoenfeld men and boys were hard at work now, beginning to build their permanent homes. Daniel was helping Abram Thielmann. There was a heap of logs waiting. Thielmann said Daniel was especially good at squaring the logs and notching them. Together they had chopped some good oak logs for the foundation and the rafters. Higher up, the walls would be of spruce and poplar.

And the weather grew warmer and warmer, the grass greener and greener, day by day. Meadow larks sang. Mother said they were nothing compared to the skylark in Russia. And she was homesick to hear the nightingale. But Cornelia loved the bubbling song of the meadowlark.

On schooldays the children played outdoors now. The boys played at knocking a tin off a stone with sticks. They played Pig in the Poke. They battered one another's ankles black and blue. Given her choice, Cornelia would have liked to be there, using a stick with the best of them. But that would never do. She played Drop the Hanky with the girls. Or *Versteck*. (Hide-and-Seek)

It was suppertime one Friday night—and Mother just sat there, not eating a thing. And yet she had gone to extra bother with supper. She had made gravy. She browned flour in a fry-pan. She poured cold water over it, and stirred it quickly to a smooth paste. She added boiling water, and brought it to a boil. Last of all she added a tablespoon of fat, and salt and pepper. At the table each placed a slice of bread in a bowl, and poured some gravy over it. And Mother wasn't eating! Father watched her anxiously.

"Now it is enough!" Mother exclaimed suddenly. "Now I am tired of living in this hole all winter. I think tomorrow we should move back to the tent."

"Isn't it a bit early?" said Father cautiously. "Cold weather may return."

"At least we'd have fresh air and sunshine."

"What is your thought, Mother?" said Father to Grandmother Siemens.

But she seldom gave advice. And when there was a decision to be made she left it to her children. "You do as you think best," was all she said.

Back to the tent, thought Cornelia. Away from this dark and smelly *simlin*. But as long as school lasted she and Father and the boys would have to walk to Schoenfeld every weekday. It was almost three miles to go.

"How long till school closes?" asked Mother with a resigned sigh.

"Another two weeks."

Daniel, who had come home just before supper, looked relieved. "Another two weeks. That will be much better."

"What will be much better?" said Mother, sounding impatient.

"To wait till then. I can—I can help you move then. That will be a good time."

In the next weeks he and Thielmann left off building the Thielmann house. From early Monday to late Saturday they were away again.

"Don't you have enough logs yet?" Cornelia asked of Huldah Thielmann. "It looks like a big pile to me."

"Well, Daniel, he and my man—they thought they would like to take out a few more logs yet."

They never brought any home though. Cornelia couldn't understand it. Why would they suddenly interrupt the work here to do something else? Not that it was any of her concern.

The final day of school came. Classes closed at noon. In the afternoon Teacher Harms and all his pupils went on an outing. Settlers had found a big rock on the prairies—a real curiosity. It was big enough for the entire school of 36 children to crowd onto. Teacher took them all to see this marvel. Their mothers had baked buns and cookies. Each pupil brought a bottle of prips. So they ate on the rock and after scrambling over it for a while they all walked back to Schoenfeld. And school was over until fall.

The very next day was moving day for the Harmses. Cornelia felt stiff from the long hike. Consequently she wasn't as spry as usual, and she felt somewhat grumpy. There were *thousands* of things for her to do. Well, *hundreds*, anyway. Or at least, *dozens*. It was Cornelia here, and Cornelia there. She was to be everybody's helper and errand boy. Sometimes two or three calls came at the same time. How could she split into three persons?

"Cornelia, come hold this while I stuff it into a bag . . . Cornelia, find my shawl . . . . Cornelia, do you remember where you packed the boys' socks? . . . . Cornelia! Cornelia! Why must I call you so often? Why don't you

159

come right away?" She wasn't the only one who was getting edgy.

And all the while Daniel was standing around, grinning and grinning to himself. What was the matter with the boy today? Cornelia was sure he was laughing at her, and this did not improve her temper one bit.

Finally a wagon load was ready. Mother couldn't wait any longer to leave the *simlin*, so they were all going with the first load. Father meant to stay, but Daniel said he might be needed at the homestead to give advice. He said it very earnestly—and then Cornelia saw him turn his back to Father and grin to himself. She was puzzled and impatient. Yet nobody else seemed to see anything strange in his actions.

The oxteam was borrowed from Thielmann. Their neighbors stood outdoors, waiting to see them off. Huldah and Little Susch were among them. They stood in the warm spring sunshine, waving. Cornelia distinctly saw Daniel and Abram Thielmann wink at each other. Something must be very wrong—or very right.

The oxen moved at their usual slow pace. Having worked so hard, none of the family felt like walking today. They perched on their goods, jolting slowly along. Occasionally Johann and Anton would jump down, run to look at something off to one side, pick a flower or two, or examine a stone. Then they came racing back to jump onto their perches again.

Daniel walked beside the team. Often he whistled snatches of song. Then he would stop abruptly. More than once Cornelia thought he was staying ahead so none could watch his face. He kept grinning and grinning. Cornelia felt she'd like to give him a good shaking.

At last they reached the homestead site. And when

160

they did, when they rounded the last bluff that had hidden the home site before, the whole family sat speechless, staring. There stood the tent, ready for them. But that wasn't the surprise. Beside the tent lay a heap of logs, large as the Thielmann's heap. All squared. Just waiting to be made into a house.

"Well!" exclaimed Father weakly. "Well, Daniel! Who did *this*?"

Daniel's face was almost splitting, he grinned so widely. But Mother's eyes were brimming with tears. She got off the wagon, and without saying a word, she went up to Daniel and hugged him. Just as if it had been Bernhard who worked secretly like this to give the family a happy home-coming surprise.

This had been Daniel's pay for the winter's work. He and Theilmann went shares, log for log. All the Schoenfeld men were in on the secret. Each time a load of logs left the forest for the village, one or two of Teacher Harms's logs was added to the load—and dropped at an agreed place a few miles away. These past two weeks the two had been busy hauling them the last few miles, so they would be ready for the surprise.

This was the story that Daniel told by degrees to a most appreciative audience. As for Cornelia, for once she couldn't find a single word to say.

VIII

First Canadian Summer

The house going up on the Harms homestead was going to have wooden floors.

In Russia one took floors for granted. But here in Canada this past winter only a fortunate few had floors other than earth. Cornelia had grown very tired of having nothing but damp earth under her feet. In the *sarais*, in *simlins*, wherever one went it was the same. People sat on the earth. They walked on it. They slept on it. So few people had enough money to buy chairs or make benches before winter closed in. And this spring many people, young and old, were hobbling around. Their joints were red and swollen. Because of the cold dampness. Early spring had been worst of all for the rheumatic people. The spring thaw sent the water seeping through the sods. It trickled down the earthen walls. It collected in puddles underfoot. Even the school *simlin* had been wet, though fortunately the Harmses had tables for bedsteads and benches for chairs.

With the help of Abram Thielmann, Cornelia's father and Daniel had laid the strong oak beams which were to be the foundation of the new home. Inside the rectangle Daniel was digging a cellar hole. It would be small and dark, but it would be a good place for potatoes, and a barrel of sauerkraut, and crockfuls of pickled pork and salt pork. Cornelia's mouth watered at the thought. One could get very, very tired of prips and bread, with a sprinkling now and then of brown sugar, or a light touch of lard with salt.

Things were moving fast this spring. This morning **Mr. Ross** came driving onto the yard with his spanking team of horses. He asked Father if he would care to go to Winnipeg with him. They could each take a wagon and return tomorrow—with enough lumber to build window frames and doorframes and the doors themselves.

Cornelia, idly stepping along the oak beams, round and round the rectangle, was startled when her grandmother called her name. Out from the tent came Grandmother, carrying a hoe and two long-handled knives.

"Cornelia! Where are your brothers?"

"Down by the creek."

"Down by the creek . . . . down by the creek! Must they always be down by the creek?"

She sounded grumpy, but she was half-joking Cornelia knew. When the boys came running, she spanked their bottoms smartly. "It is time you go to work too. Johann, Daniel can use your help. Why are you so lazy? Get busy and carry that heap of earth away."

"Where shall I carry it to?"

"Anywhere! Think of a place, a good place. Must we always do your thinking for you? How will your father put a floor in the house if there is a big pile of earth in the middle?"

The boys laughed. They imagined the house with a humpy floor, and pretended to be climbing hills and sliding down into valleys in getting from one room to another. As soon as Daniel could make himself heard he suggested that Johann should carry the earth to the edges of the rectangle, and pile it up against the oak beams. That way it would help to keep the house warm.

"Do you hear, Johann?" said Grandmother. "Now make yourself useful. And Cornelia and Anton, I need you in the garden."

163

Of course, there was no garden anywhere around—except in Grandmother's lively mind. But last fall, while they lived in the tent here, their neighbor Ross had ploughed a fireguard around their yard. After he warned them of the danger of grass fires, Father had burnt off a square of grass. But that had not satisfied their neighbor. One day he brought his team and plough. The square was surrounded by a ploughed strip now. And Grandmother intended to make this earth into a garden.

The grass and roots were half rotted in their trenches by now. Grandmother stooping over her hoe, and the children on their knees with knives, began chopping the sods, cutting them fine, then rubbing the earth finer still between their hands. It was slow, tiring work. Grandmother who ought to be most tired, kept reminding them of the vegetables they would be eating in a few months' time. She pretended they were out here, picking peas and beans, and pulling carrots and onions. And digging up potatoes. And picking handfuls of summer savory and parsley. Indoors, in their new home, Mother would have a ham boiling. And they would sit on the shady side of the house, shelling the peas and washing the other vegetables.

"Can't you almost taste the soup?"

"But where will we get the cream?" said Anton seriously.

"Oh, by then we'll have a cow. She will be eating the grass that grows to her shoulders. Think of it, children. Butter, and cream, and milk! And Mother said she will try soon to get some chickens, so we'll have eggs too."

After the fireguard was all chopped up and rubbed fine and raked smooth and seeded, other jobs were waiting. Grandmother's garden project took two weeks. Two weeks of long, hard days. Cornelia's mother had not been able to help. She was too busy with other jobs, particularly with feeding workmen.

New immigrants were arriving every week or so at the Schanz shelters. Two of them, men who had been builders in Russia, had offered to help Teacher Harms. Their own group of farmers who would be forming a village with them were still on the way somewhere. Until their arrival, they could not decide where to settle. And merely waiting was tiring work, they said. They might as well be doing something useful.

So the walls of the house-barn went up fast. The house had eight-foot walls, like those of all the Mennonite homes. The barn walls rose four feet higher. When they were finished, some men came over from Schoenfeld to help raise the roof beams. Everyone, even Daniel, knew exactly what to do, it seemed.

Neighbor Ross stood watching that day.

"Now *this* I like!" he remarked to Teacher Harms. "This is cooperation and self-help at its best."

Cornelia who had overheard saw her father's eyes twinkle. "Oh, I would not say so. We Mennonites help each other, yes. Because we need each other. We give, and we receive. But when my neighbor who is not of my people gives me help and more help, and I can give nothing in return—"

"Don't think it for a minute, Peter."

"Will you tell me just one thing that I have given you?"

Ronald Ross laughed. "An education. An eye-opener." And he rode off toward his homestead.

After the roof-raising came thatching, and that was where the womenfolk took over. In fact, they had already spent some days at the job. All day Cornelia and her mother and grandmother cut dry grass stalks and tied them into small bundles. They had to keep working steadily to remain ahead of the man who was tying layers of bundles down. Thousands and thousands of bundles . . Sawing stalks until your back was one ache, and all your blood seemed to be thundering in your head. And hurrying, hurrying all the time.

When the roof over the barn area was thatched, the Harmses moved in there. The floor was earthen still. They could keep making and using open fires. They could have fresh air. But they were sheltered from the hot sun, and from most of the chill winds and the rain. And they had room. It was a great improvement over the tent and the *simlin*.

The windows were still nothing more than holes in the walls, here as well as in the house area. The only inside wall that was finished was the one that would divide the house from the barn. But they were living in their own home. For the first time since Peter and Sarah Harms were married they were living in their own home!

Cornelia's mother walked about, her eyes shining. Already she knew how the rooms would look—the Big Room, the Corner room, the Middle Room, the Summer room, the entry, the pantry, the kitchen . . . All Mennonite homes were built more or less according to one pattern.

The core of the house—its heart—was the built-in brick stove. The two men were busy building it now. It would form the wall dividing the Big Room from the Middle Room, so that most of the house could be kept snug and warm in winter. The stove needed no metal pipes through which the smoke could escape. Above the stove, in the attic of the house, there would be a wide boxy space lined with boards. It was walled off from the rest of the attic. The chimney of the house sat squarely above this space. The smoke, issuing from the flue of the stove, swirled through the boxy space and out through the chimney. In fall there would be sausages and bacon sides and hams hanging in that area. It was an easy way to smoke meats and keep them from spoiling.

The rafters of the house and barn were strong beams—seven inches by seven. They had to be strong, because the upstairs area of a house served as granary. When Farmer Harms harvested his crops in fall, there would be heaps of grain up there. *If the land got ploughed as it ought to.*

That was one thing that had not gone exactly to plan. Perhaps the Schoenfeld farmers had had too much to do, breaking their own land and building their homes. Most of them seemed to forget that they had promised Teacher Harms the breaking and harrowing of an acre of land. It was time to do the seeding. Neighbor Ross had offered to sell enough grain, barley, oats and wheat to seed twenty acres. But only five of the twenty were ready for seeding.

"So the system has broken down, has it?" said Neighbor Ross. "You can't clothe and feed a family of six on five acres of land. Not in this part of the world."

"Five acres are better than no acres," said Teacher Harms meekly. He did not criticize a fellow Mennonite to an outsider.

Grandmother Siemens had prepared a seeding bag for him. She knew about such things, having grown up on a farm. She could still demonstrate how to pace steadily, and swing your arm rhythmically, scattering the seed. So it would fall in even sweeps.

The bag had a strap that went over one shoulder and under the other arm. It was Cornelia's job to keep filling the bag as Father emptied it. It was his to pace the acres, scattering the seed.

When the five acres were seeded, Daniel helped to drag a heavy oaken beam over the furrows so as to cover the seeds. Usually he worked in Schoenfeld now. He had a new job. Abram Thielmann had opened a little store. He said he had found Daniel so trustworthy he wanted no one else to help him. Daniel's job included frequent trips to Winnipeg to haul home goods for the store.

It seemed a marvel to Johann and Anton that Daniel knew so much about the city of Winnipeg. There were seventeen hotels in Winnipeg, he told them. And twenty-three rooming houses. And twenty-seven factories. And seven saloons —

Grandmother, who had overheard the talk, gave Daniel a very level look. "Only that you don't begin to keep bad company in that big city of yours," she said.

He got red. "I don't. And I won't," he said.

"See to it," said Grandmother gravely.

Daniel used horses on those trips. That in itself made his job exciting. And his daily wages had risen to fifty cents. That was as much as a full-grown miller would earn in a day. And Daniel was only fifteen.

Every Saturday when he came home he told of new things happening in Schoenfeld or in some of the other new villages. Most of them were built along the banks of a stream, and most of the streams flowed north-west. So the one main street of most villages ran from southeast to northwest. Winding roads connected village to village now, all through the settlement. People visited back and forth, so news got around. About windmills that were being built—mills for grinding grain, and for sawing logs into lumber. About stores that were being opened. About the coming of new settlers who had brought money with them from Russia. This was especially cheering news.

The first Bergthalers to leave Russia last year had had to leave before their homes and land were paid for. This year's immigrants had brought part of the purchase price with them. And in a few months they would be selling their first crop. Things should be easier for the settlers soon.

"How much money do we get?" asked Anton Harms, when the family was discussing these matters.

"Money from Russia?" said Johann scornfully. "What are you thinking? *We* never had any land. How could we get any money?"

Grandmother smoothed Anton's stand-up hair, because he was feeling embarrassed. "Never mind. Never mind. We have a home now. Soon we will be having our own crops too. When you and Johann are old enough, you can take up your own homestead. So there'll be three times as much land to farm."

"But I don't want to be a farmer," objected Johann promptly. "I want to be a builder. A worker with machinery."

Johann and his dreams. He still often spoke about the locks on the Great Lakes.

"We'll see. We'll see," said Father mildly. "It is not a simple thing to learn to be an engineer. That costs money. And that money—if it comes—will have to come from the farm. Have a little patience."

You always came back to the same point: money. The Harmses had never had much. Before leaving Russia Peter Harms borrowed money from the *Oberschulze*.

169

Most of that had melted away by now. As teacher he had earned $65.00 for the winter's work—besides the promise of getting twenty acres ploughed this spring. They all felt gloomy at the thought of the fifteen unploughed acres. Where was the money to come from to repay their debt to the *Oberschulze*?

"Neighbor Ross says it's almost too late now, except for greenfeed," said Peter Harms sadly. "Frost comes early here."

In the late sunshine, the whole family stood outside, looking over the seeded five acres. The young wheat looked good, very good. So did the fire-guard garden that formed a collar around the yard. There had been a few showers. The ferny carrots were showing. The tender spears of onions stood in soldierly rows. Green rosettes of potato leaves hugged the ground. Beans were popping up, each wearing its mother bean like a shrivelled bonnet.

"It's good, good soil," said Father smiling. "We can be thankful for that."

Each day now, the Harms' well was being dug. One of the new settlers, George Pilatus, had stayed to build the wood cribbing. Peter Harms and Daniel took turns in going down into the well to do the digging. Twenty feet . . . . thirty . . . forty . . . The deeper they went, the deeper went the cribbing. There must be no cave-in here. Still, no water came up. But something else did.

It had become the chore of Cornelia to pull up the loose earth. Pilatus had erected a pulley wheel over which the rope ran that lowered the empty pails and brought up the full ones. Once, in her hurry (her arms were getting awfully tired) Cornelia dropped the empty pail too fast. It slammed down on her father's head. She tried to stop it, just too late.

170

"Ow-weh!" His protesting groan came floating up. "What are you *thinking*, child?"

"I—I'm sorry. I will be more careful."

Yet a few minutes later she let a whole pailful of earth go swinging down to the well bottom again. Her father got out of its way just in time.

"Father! Father!" she quavered. "Are you hurt?"

"No. But that's not to your credit. Maybe it's time you have a rest. I'm coming up now."

There were steps nailed to the cribbing. He came climbing up. Then he took charge of the rope. Cornelia watched, fascinated. The earth had been white—all white. It had taken her so much by surprise, she had failed to grasp the handle properly.

"What is it?" she asked when the load came to the surface.

"White clay. We'll use it to whitewash our home, inside and out. That will please your mother."

But before that could be done, the log walls had to be caulked. And that was another job for the women folk. As soon as Pilatus had the windows and doors in place, the caulking could begin. They used clay from the well, and water from the creek. They spread the earth in a circular layer. When it had been moistened, they took off shoes and stockings, and began treading the clay. Grandmother, Mother, Cornelia, Johann and Anton— Sometimes they held hands and swung in circles. Sometimes they trod singly. Even though the weather was warm, the mud seemed very cold. It squeezed between one's toes. It slopped up around one's ankles. It was slithery work, especially at first. But gradually the clay became stickier and stickier. More and more of it clung to their feet. Each leg seemed to be weighted with ten pounds of mud.

171

When that part of the job was done, it was time to begin filling the cracks between the logs with clay. But first they all ran to the creek to wash their feet and ankles. Drying clay on your skin can be horribly itchy.

Grandmother sat down on the grassy bank. She let the children pour water over her feet. But Mother stepped into the creek, and began paddling around, laughing like any young girl.

"I used to do this—in the Molotschna," she called breathlessly to Grandmother. "Do you remember?"

"How should I not remember?"

"And we used to do this in the Bodena," said Cornelia. Suddenly she and her mother were grave. "We" meant Cornelia and Bernhard. Brother and sister, almost always together.

"I'm lonesome for the Bodena—and for the hill behind it—and for—for—"

"Bernhard," finished her mother softly.

It was a long time since they had talked about him. In months they had almost never been alone, even for a moment. The boys were teasing Grandmother by sloshing more and more water over her feet when she was trying to dry them. She was laughing, and pleading, and threatening. Together they made enough noise to make this creek a very private place for a talk.

"Do *you* miss him too?" said Cornelia wistfully.

"Ach, yes. And you?"

"Terribly, terribly—especially at times. But sometimes I forget. And then I'm ashamed and more sad than ever. To think I could forget him!"

"You need not be ashamed, child. We couldn't live if yesterday's sorrows always remained a fresh hurt. Being able to forget in time is one of God's great gifts."

172

"Oh, I couldn't. I couldn't forget."

"Not completely. Never that. But gradually it becomes less and less."

"Well, does your homesickness for Russia grow less too?"

"It will. It must. We have a new home now. We are putting down roots in this new land."

But Cornelia noticed sorrowfully that her mother had not said, "It is growing less." Simply, "It will. It must." Could you simply make up your mind not to feel hurt?

"*Frisch an's Werk*," called Grandmother (back to work). "What are you two so serious about?"

In the next hours their hands grew as sticky as their feet had been. But it was nice to know that they would have a snug, snug home next winter. Snug and roomy, and sunny. No more *simlin* darkness and dampness for the Harms family!

Two indoor walls were ready for their coating of mud too. These had to have mud that had a grass binding. It meant more trampling of mud—and sometimes the children grew grumpy over it.

"Hui-jui!" called their grandmother one day. "You should be proud of this work. One day you will tell your grandchildren how you helped to build a house, your new home in Canada. *Frisch an's Werk!*"

Sometimes Cornelia wondered what ever the Harms family would have done if Grandmother had not decided to come with them. Father and Mother got discouraged at times. Not Grandmother. Or if she did, no one ever found out.

The day Father came into the barn area where Mother was making potato soup Cornelia knew instantly that something was wrong. His face was pale. He walked waveringly, as though he were sick.

"Come, see," he said.

"What has happened."

"Come, see."

All of them trooped after him, across the yard.

"Listen! Can't you hear?"

"What is it? What is it?"

"Come, see."

He led them to the nearest edge of the fire-guard garden.

"My carrots! My peas! Where are they?" wailed Grandmother. "What's happened?"

They were gone. Where the vegetables had stood in proud young rows, there was nothing now but black earth. And beyond that, the wheat was fast disappearing. Grasshoppers, millions of grasshoppers, had invaded the field and settled on all the stalks of green.

"I thought—it was—a misfortune," said Father jerkily, "That the Schoenfeld—men—forgot to plough—my acres. They have—at least—saved me—the price of seed grain."

This is death. This is another kind of dying, thought Cornelia wildly. *Oh, I want to go back—back to Russia.*

Instead, they all went back to their waiting potato soup. Mother served it in silence. They sat down in silence. Even Anton had no question to ask today. When they bowed their heads for prayer, there was a silence for a long moment too. Then Father spoke shakily, "The Lord hath given, the Lord hath taken away. Blest be the name of the Lord. Amen!"

Cornelia often thought of that prayer in the weeks that followed. There were grasshoppers in the house, grasshoppers in the well, grasshoppers in the creek, grass-hoppers on the yard. They rustled and they crunched under your feet. No one wanted to go barefoot. Father hastily made a pair of *Schlore* (wooden sandals) for each. You killed grasshoppers with every step you took, but you didn't have to feel the squishy, metallic things under the naked soles of your feet. And no matter how many were killed, there were millions and millions more. The whole settlement was hit by the plague. They faced a bleak winter. Many of the settlers said aloud what Cornelia had thought silently, "I want to go back."

But it was a fruitless wish even for them. They had spent most of their money to make the move. There was nothing left for a return to their old home—and no homes waiting for them to go to there.

Peter Harms borrowed a horse and buggy to take his family for a ride one day—a ride through the settlement. Cornelia wanted most of all to have a visit with her Suschki. But Father didn't drive directly to Schoenfeld. They made a wide loop through the area. Some fields were planned in *Streifenfluren*. Some were not. In some villages each farmer farmed his own quarter of land, just as the *Englaender* neighbors did. But whether the fields were in strips or rectangles, it made no difference. All the ploughed land was patchy at best, completely bald most everywhere.

The air was filled with the whirring, spitting creatures. They whirled down on you. They spit at your clothes, and each jet of spit left a tiny hole. The horses grew impatient with the flying pests. They snorted, tossing their heads as they trotted on. The Harmses mostly sat in depressed silence.

They drove through village after village. Everywhere

people were building houses and barns. Or thatching roofs. Or digging wells. Or building picket fences. Some of the men stopped work when they saw Teacher Harms. Everyone knew him because he was the secretary at the *Schulzenbott*. They came to lean over picket fences, to talk seriously about the settlement and what it ought to do. There was to be a general meeting of the men soon. They would have to find a way. They would probably be borrowing money somewhere to see them through next winter.

Cornelia noticed one thing. After their first greeting, the men did not look one another in the eye. Their glances slid away, across one another's shoulders. They spoke in subdued voices as people do in the presence of death. Each seemed to be saying, *We're here. There's no help for it. We must make the best of things. With the help of God.*

As if on signal, they would raise their hands in a farewell salute. Father clucked to the team. The men went back to their work. The Harmses drove on.

At 12 o'clock they arrived in Schoenfeld, at the Thielmann door. Here their greeting was so hearty that it seemed almost noisy in comparison. Huldah Thielmann had dinner waiting. Best of all, Suschki was awake. Cornelia could play with her to her heart's content. She was a lively, bouncy baby now, and even the boys became interested in playing with her.

For once the grasshoppers were hardly mentioned, though you could hear them crashing against the shutters and the window panes every moment. The grownups talked about Russia. About Agatha and Wilhelm and the baby. About Huldah and Abram's relatives and friends. Every letter from Agatha was like a song with a one-word chorus that was repeated over and over. *Bernhardki, Bernhardki!* Wilhelm had taken him for a ride on horseback, and he had crowed with delight. All the servants were so fond of him. Everybody spoiled the little *Liebling*. Grandfather Franz was the worst of all in this.

After dinner Father set out to visit Schoenfeld people, and he took the boys with him. Grandmother, Mother, and Cornelia brought out their knitting. Huldah Thielmann got out her darning. (Her man was such a one to get holes in his socks!) And Suschki lay in her cradle, murmuring to herself, almost asleep. A string from the cradle ran to Huldah's great toe. At a slight twitch the cradle began rocking gently. For the baby's sake the conversation was hushed, too.

Huldah was lonesome for home. She spoke of her parents, sisters and brothers in Russia. She was glad for her new home, for in Russia they had been landless. She loved her baby. She was proud of the fact that her Abram had opportunities here that he never could have had in Russia. Look at the way he and Daniel worked last winter. All that wood they could cut down free! Look at the store he had opened. He had had to borrow money, but he was paying it back quickly. Her Abram had never regretted his decision to come to a new land, never for a moment. But she ached for the sight of home faces, the sound of home voices.

"When I think that I will never see them again . . ." Her voice broke.

"In heaven we will. We can be glad that we have this assurance," said Mother soothingly.

Huldah dried her eyes. "How can we be sure?" she

burst out. "I want them *here, now.* How can I be sure I'll get to heaven, even?"

"Why, Huldah, Huldah!"

Cornelia's heart quivered. She knew exactly how Huldah felt. These were questions that often tortured her. *How could one be sure?*

"I spoke to Ohm Sawatsky the other day. I asked him the same questions," Huldah went on broodingly.

"And what did he say?"

"He said we must hope—and keep on hoping. He said we must hope that the grace of God will be great enough to cover our sins. He said that all of us are great sinners—and I know it. I know I am. But how can I know that hoping will be enough?"

"It won't," said Mother quietly.

Cornelia's heart turned over. Huldah was staring at Sarah Harms in surprise and fear.

"Never?"

"Never."

"No, no," murmured Grandmother. "No, no."

"Well then—"

"Hope is not enough," Cornelia heard her mother say firmly. "But God's grace is. Where God's promises are concerned there is no place for a trembling hope. There is only *knowing.*"

Sarah Harms's face was alight. "God has said, 'whosoever will, let him take of the water of life, *freely.*' He has said, 'But as many as received Him, to them gave he the right to be called the sons of God.' His Word says, 'We *know* that we have passed from death into life . . .' There is a *knowing.* There is a *knowing.*"

"But—but if this is so, why don't our *Ohms* preach it on Sundays?"

178

"They do. It is all there—all there in their sermons. They use the Bible, and it is all there. It is the Word of God."

"But—"

"But somewhere—somehow, many of our people seem to have lost the way. My man says that there is God's part to salvation, and there is our part. God's part was done when Jesus died for our sins. He paid the price, the *full* price. On the cross He called out, *It is finished.* Now He invites: *Come. Take. Believe. It is free.* And our part is to take it. For ourselves. Then it is ours, and we may *know* that it is ours, and that we stand in the grace of God."

"Sarah Harms, I have never known these things before."

Huldah Thielmann was laughing and she was crying. She wiped her eyes on the great grey sock of her man. They were still sitting in a circle. Knitting and darning needles were busy. Huldah's great toe still twitched now and then, and the obedient cradle rocked gently from side to side. Everything still the same. But Cornelia sensed that something mystifying had happened to Huldah.

"I think—I think I've come Home—to God," she said in an awed whisper.

The change in Sarah Harms was just as great. Peter Harms noticed it the moment he stepped through the door. His eyes lit up, and he stood straighter than Cornelia had seen him stand in many months, it seemed. He had intended to take them straight home, but Huldah begged them to stay for an early *Vaspa* (mid-afternoon refreshments.) After that they drove homeward across the scarred prairies.

They drove singing. Father had caught the mood from

179

Mother and Grandmother. They sang, *Ich habe nun den Grund gefunden . . ."* (Now I have found the Ground) They sang about Jesus' death on the cross. They sang about looking forward to heaven. They sang about how Jesus was their daily companion in life.

The grasshoppers still whirred through the air. If you weren't careful, they came whirling right into your open mouth. It almost happened to Mother. One crashed against her teeth. But even this did not stop her. She sang on.

Their roof dipped up out of the sea of grass. Home. It was home—in spite of the wasted acres. Two Schoenfeld farmers were busy breaking up more acres of sod on the Harms homestead.

There would be other years, other crops.

IX
A People of their Word

Even though the grasshoppers had chewed up the crops, there were some improvements in the settlement that fall of 1875. The people were living in houses now, instead of the damp dark dens of the winter before. Most of them, that is. Some families remained in their *simlins* for as long as six years.

Sheds were full of chopped firewood. Haylofts held summer-cured hay. Barns were beginning to house livestock. A few chickens, perhaps, and a piglet or two. A cow or two for the milk and butter needs of the family. But the storage area above the family home held no binfuls of vegetables and grain. And there was no money to buy any. The settlement would have to make a loan, just to remain alive. The question was, Who was there who would be rich enough to lend $96,000 to the poor settlers?

The leading men had to do some figuring. And $96,000 was the minimum for their needs in food and livestock and implements. It was the government of Canada that had invited them to come to this country. So why not go to the government for a loan, promising to repay it all with interest?

There were grumbles in Parliament when the request was made. The government wasn't in the lending business, people said. What if *everyone*, every immigrant came with a similar request? What if the money would not be repaid?

Still, the Mennonites got the loan. This was a story that was told and retold often that bleak winter. It was like a fire to warm not only one's body but one's heart. How one of the great men in Parliament got to his feet to speak for the new settlers. The trouble they were in was not their fault. They had come to Canada in good faith, but had suffered a complete crop failure. They were people to be trusted. They were thrifty and hard-working. All the world knew Mennonites were people of their word. If they promised to repay the loan, they would repay it. And they would repay it with interest.

(And, 17 years later, when the loan had been paid in full, there were speeches again in Parliament. *See? They did it! They said they would, and they did it!* They returned more than $130,000 for the $96,000 loan. Such a thing had never happened in Canada's history.)

The money was spent first of all in buying sufficient meat and flour and beans. Some was set aside for machinery and livestock. There still was no money for clothes.

The ones they had brought with them from Russia were threadbare and tattered. Mothers ripped up cotton and burlap bags to sew aprons and shirts and underwear— but they provided little warmth. Men and boys often wore their Sunday suits under their patched overalls and workshirts on weekdays. On Sundays the overalls and suits changed places.

Teacher Harms's family had one great problem that they had not had the previous winter. They lived three miles from school now. They had bought a two-seater buggy. But they had no horses and no sleigh. Cornelia's father told her that she and Anton would simply have to miss school on the very cold days. Johann was such a husky Siemens in build, a daily six-mile walk might not hurt him.

But Cornelia saw her mother look at Father and shake her head silently. The look said, But *you* can't walk it.

It was their *Englaender* neighbor, Ronald Ross, who solved the problem for them. He offered them the use of a team.

"Not a spry team, I warn you. Well past their prime, as horses go. But I know they'll still beat an oxteam any day. And you'd be doing me a favor, Peter, if you made use of them. Reduce my chores this winter. Keep the old crocks from stiffening up."

Peter Harms's eyes twinkled. He knew his neighbor by now—knew that he always managed to make his offers of help sound like a favor to himself. Still, Harms shook his head regretfully. Horses needed grain now and then. He had nothing but hay in his barn.

"Oh, I'd be feeding them oats at home. Might as well let you do that little job for me."

And, true to his word, he came the next day, Saturday, he and his little son Derek. The entire Harms family watched the horses being led into their new stall—next to Brindle the cow. One was a long-necked white, named Lanky. The other, a dirty brown, went by the name of Scott.

"What do you think of them?" Ronald Ross said, tapping Anton's head.

"They are not pretty," said the boy.

"Anton!" Mother was shocked and embarrassed. But their neighbor only laughed. "Handsome is as handsome does," he said. "They will serve you faithfully."

"That handsome is as handsome does" was an *Englaender* proverb Father explained later. It meant that if you

183

behave beautifully, you *are* beautiful—even if you look plain. But if you act ugly, you are really ugly, no matter how beautiful you may look. The horses would look very, very beautiful to Anton on the first frosty morning when they saved him a grim walk to Schoenfeld.

Next morning, Sunday, the whole family drove to church in the buggy, drawn by Lanky and Scott. (*Englaender* people gave their horses funny names.) The sky was grey as lead, and a cold wind blew. Just when they entered Schoenfeld they passed an oxcart. A girl sat alone on the seat, all wrapped in buffalo skins. A young man walked beside his oxen.

"Isaac Elias!" exclaimed Father softly.

"And Annie Falk," said Mother just as softly. "So there is to be a wedding today after all."

Both were poor orphans. But Annie had, for several years, been hired girl in the home of one of the richest Bergthaler couples, the Dietrich Jantzens. She worked for them in Russia. She accompanied them to Canada. All Schoenfeld knew the story of how a young man of 19 came to propose to Annie, who was 18 now. And how the Jantzens tried to put a stop to the matter. But both Annie and Isaac longed to have a home of their own. Isaac had a homestead, on which he had built a small log house. Evidently they had won their point.

The Jantzens had chosen this day to pay a visit to another village. There were no relations, no special friends, to sit with the young bride in church. Annie, wearing a shabby dress of brown flannelette, sat quietly alone—until Sarah Harms took Cornelia with her to sit in the same bench. Annie smiled at them, but her eyes sidled proudly again to Isaac. In new denim overalls and knee-high felt boots he sat directly across the aisle from her.

184

Cornelia, remembering the splendor of Agatha's black wedding dress, thought what a shame it was that Annie could not come to her wedding in decent black. Mrs. Jantzen could have afforded to sew a new dress for her. They were rich enough. Annie deserved it. But—maybe—she was happy enough without it, though Cornelia couldn't *quite* see what she saw in Isaac Elias.

It was Ohm Peters' turn to preach this morning, and Cornelia was glad. So, she felt sure, were all the young people in church. Of all the preachers in Schoenfeld, he was the most cheerful one.

Each Sunday—as in Russia—all the *Ohms* came in together. They went to sit in a dignified row on the long narrow platform. Each Sunday two of them preached. Their sermons were mostly taken from learned books of sermons. Father said they were good sermons—but deep. Cornelia could understand most of the words, but she had an advantage. The Harms family regularly spoke High German at home. But most of the young people spoke it only in school. At home, and while talking with one another, they slipped into one of the Lowland dialects. Usually the two-hour Sunday morning service seemed very, very long. It was different when Ohm Peters' turn came though.

He spoke last, just before the wedding ceremony. Even his text was interesting and different. "Oh thou of little faith! Wherefore didst thou doubt?"

You could see he had the bride and groom in mind, though he did not mention them particularly. But then, he was talking to all Schoenfeld, too, to the whole settlement! He reminded them of last winter—and of all the events since their coming to Canada. At the mention of last winter Cornelia's thought slipped away. She saw

185

the dark *simlin*—the windowless kitchen— the beds made up on school tables. This winter she and Grandmother had a room to themselves, and a bed made of wood and of woven strips of raw cowhide. Their room was always cosily warm.

She and Mother and Grandmother had braided last year's ragged clothes into rugs for the plank floor. They were so pretty and homelike. The walls were all whitewashed. Compared with last year's den, their homes looked bright and cheerful. But there was one thing missing—confident hope.

Last year, through all the cold, dark days, the settlers had kept thinking. Wait. Wait till spring. It's coming. Spring sunshine. Spring warmth. With spring will come new life for all. We'll work hard. We'll seed the acres. We'll harvest the crops. Next fall we'll have vegetables to store for winter's use. We'll have meat and milk and eggs to eat.

Now "next winter" was here. Cellars and granaries were empty. Bodies shivered in threadbare clothing, and people dreaded to think of the colder months ahead. Stomachs growled because of the coarse bread that still was almost their only daily food. And there were doubts and fears about the future.

What if next summer should be a repetition of the last one? What if this country never yielded any crops? What if they could not keep their promise to the government? What then?

"Are these your thoughts this morning?" said Ohm Peters. "Then it is to you I say, 'Is God dead? Is His arm shortened that He cannot save?' Must Jesus say to us, as He said to His disciples on earth, 'O fools, and slow of heart to believe . . .' And again, 'Oh, thou of little faith, wherefore didst thou doubt?' "

More now than ever, said Ohm Peters, they needed faith—and faith—and more faith. Faith in God who never yet broke His word to anyone!

"That was a fine sermon for a wedding," remarked Grandmother Siemens on the way home.

"A fine sermon for everyone," said Peter Harms.

"I have heard— Mrs. Peters told me—" said Mother, sounding indignant, "that the Jantzens are not giving Anna an *Utstia*. They promised it. Always they said that as part of her wages, they would give her all the bedding she would need when she married. Now they say no. She married Elias. She chose a poor man. So let them be poor together."

Snowflakes were coming down, soft and thick. As if, thought Cornelia, as if someone had emptied a sky-sized feather-tick into the air. One could not breathe without snuffing up a few cold feathers. The oxcart bearing the newly married pair was behind them again. Cornelia swung round for a quick look. This time both were seated, wrapped in buffalo skins. Snowflakes wrapped them round too. It must seem a very private ride.

Cornelia's mother invited them to share the Harms's Sunday dinner.

"I cannot give you a real wedding dinner. But let me take the place of a mother as well as I can today," she said. And shyly, Anna asked her Isaac and they were coming.

The Harmses arrived home an hour ahead of their guests, of course. Sarah Harms added water and a bit of cream to the Sunday borscht. For an added treat she took a few patties of aged cottage cheese out of the bag

187

that hung beside the stove. This was one of the good things about having a cow. You could make cheese. The cakes were made of curds with salt and butter added, and with dill seed. They had been shaped into patties and dried hard as hard could be. Done this way, they kept a long, long time. Mother grated the cheese so it could be strewed over bread and butter. Then she got a plateful of syrup cookies out of the pantry. They were to have been eaten at *Vaspa*. But a wedding dinner was special. One should have special foods—even if the bride and groom were friendless orphans.

They were very quiet at the table, very shy. Isaac Elias hardly spoke at all. And as soon as dinner was over he went out to yoke up his oxen again.

Sarah Harms had packed a loaf of bread, a few cookies and a pat of butter into a basket for the bride to carry to her new home. But her special gift to the young homemaker was two needles, bright and new. A darning needle and one for ordinary sewing. Needles were very precious and scarce. No wonder the bride's face lit up.

"Oh, you are too good to me—too good to me," she said, choking up. "I will take such care of them."

"Poor children!" murmured Sarah Harms. "That Maria Jantzen! Someone should tell her something! Casting Anna off like that!"

"Of the two I pity Mrs. Jantzen most," remarked Peter Harms. "Well, it looks outside as if winter has really come."

The winter proved to be neither as long nor as severe as the one before. With Lanky and Scott to take the Harmses to school every day, Cornelia kept on attending, though she was the oldest girl in school now. Few girls went beyond their thirteenth birthday. In learning,

Cornelia had outstripped the others of her age long ago. She was smaller than two of the 12-year-olds, so she did not look out of place. Her father tutored her alone. When he wanted her to read books other than the accepted school texts, she did so at home—and she wrote her assignments in school. It worked out happily for everybody.

She might have remained at home and studied there. In some ways it would have been pleasanter. At home Father was—*Father*. On the way to school, too. But the moment they arrived at school he was Teacher Harms, not easy to approach.

It was little Suschki who kept Cornelia in school this winter. How else could she run in and out at the Thielmann's every day, and watch the baby growing and learning. She seemed to be learning new skills every day. In her long dress she looked like a little old woman. Cornelia thought there was nothing cuter in all the world than that baby. Unless it might be Bernhardki in the Molotschna colony. But he was so far away. She would never get to know him.

Teachers in all Mennonite villages had a position of power. If a pupil got a whipping in school, he was sure to get another at home—just for having been naughty enough to deserve punishment. (Of *course*, he deserved it—if Teacher said he did. Teacher was always right.) And where Teacher had a sense of justice the pupils respected him all the more for being strict. But there was another kind of teacher. Cornelia heard about one when the Harmses made a trip to *"Jant Sied"*—(the other side)—west of the Red River.

Sarah Harms had heard with excitement one day that a very dear childhood friend of hers had come to Canada with her family last fall. The David Schapanskys had settled west of the Red. As soon as the snow had disappeared in spring, before the frost had quite left the ground so spring work could commence, the Peter Harms family paid a visit to the Schapansky homestead.

That year, 1876, the Canadian government passed an Order in Council which set aside 17 townships west of the river for Mennonites. Even before that, many Mennonites had trickled west. Because, as Ronald Ross had foreseen, the east reserve simply was not suited to *Streifenfluren*. Those settlers who wanted to stick to old customs found the west reserve more suited to their purpose. Many villages sprang up overnight.

But there were many single Mennonite homesteads too. The David Schapanskys lived on one of these. The man and two almost grownup sons were busy preparing next winter's fuel when the Harmses arrived. One couldn't stop in the middle of a job like that.

It was like being transported back to Russia. The west reserve did not have trees for firewood. You had to travel all day to the Pembina hills if you wished to chop down trees. But Mennonites were used to doing without firewood.

In the warm spring sunshine, Cornelia perched on a fence rail beside Liesbet, her new friend. Liesbet was a year younger than Cornelia, who had just turned 14. She was larger than Cornelia, and fair-haired, and freckled. In looks they were opposites. But within minutes of their meeting they had discovered that they were alike in other things. Both were lively and quick. They laughed at the same things. Both were fond of outdoor activities. Their mothers agreed that it was disgraceful for two girls as

190

old as they to behave like children—but even the mothers laughed when they said it.

Liesbet's father and big brother had spread a deep bed of barnyard manure in a large circle; all the manure that had collected through the winter. They spread hay over the area, then poured water over it. Now they were driving a team of horses round and round through the manure, kneading it thoroughly.

After that it would be partially dried, and cut into bricks. These would be turned and dried some more. Later the bricks would be piled into pyramids. And when they were quite, quite dry, they would be stored for winter's use. By then they would have no odor at all. It was clean, hot fuel, and it left very little ash.

Even now, mixed with sunshine and fresh air, the smell was not disagreeable. In any case, the new friends were too busy gossiping and giggling to be offended by a few strong whiffs. Naturally they compared schools.

Her teacher was strict, *terribly* strict, said Liesbet. He had queer notions. Every girl had to wear an apron every day. If she came without one, he sent her back home. Every boy was supposed to wear a jacket with a sailor collar. But some of the mothers were dissatisfied with that rule, because it was they who had to do the sewing. Teacher had drawn a chalk line down the middle of the room. The boys had to keep to one side of that line, the girls to the other. If the toe of your shoe so much as *touched* the line you were punished.

"No! How? Does he—does he *whip* you?"

"Not the girls. He makes us sit on a bench, facing the corner. He says we must shame ourselves there. Everybody is glad he isn't going to teach next year."

"How do you know?"

Liesbet giggled. "He isn't married," she explained. "So he eats with the village families, a week at each home." She was laughing so heartily she almost tumbled from her perch.

"And?" urged Cornelia, giving her arm an impatient shake.

"One of the mothers, Mrs. Klass Dueck, found out that he doesn't like soup. She told the others. So all winter, wherever he ate, he got soup, soup, and nothing but soup. For breakfast, even. So he has said he does not want to teach us any longer."

They giggled together, although Cornelia had a fleeting thought about how the teacher must feel.

"Are you going back to school?"

"What do you *think*? exclaimed Liesbet, astonished. "I'm *thirteen*!"

Cornelia asked soberly, "Do you think—sometimes—of what is coming next?"

Liesbet dimpled and blushed. "Sometimes. And you?"

"Sometimes," admitted Cornelia.

Thirteen and fourteen were great ages, when you stopped to think of it. A few more years—and so much to learn. How to be a homemaker— how to bake bread and buns. How to cook food. How to make butter and keep a dairy clean. How to make sauerkraut and pickles. How to make a garden and keep it clean. How to raise chickens and geese, calves and piglets. How to make soap. How to make quilts and comforters. How to card wool, and spin it, and knit it into stockings and caps, mittens and sweaters and scarves. How to sew men's shirts and trousers. How to keep a house clean. How to make a home. A few years for all the hundreds of howtos! After that a Mennonite girl was thought to be ready to become a wife and mother.

192

"But what if—nobody *wants* us?" Liesbet whispered the awful thought. And even Cornelia's heart trembled at the words. "You don't have to be afraid," Liesbet went on consolingly. "You are pretty."

"I? What are you *saying!*" But her protest was only half honest. Of late her tiny mirror had been telling her new things, comforting things, about her face.

"Pretty and nice. I have two older brothers. I'll tell them how nice you are."

Insured against being an Old Maid—almost the worst thing that could happen to a Mennonite girl—Cornelia followed her friend indoors to see what their mothers were up to. It was *Vaspa* time. The men had unhitched the team. The manure had been kneaded to the proper consistency, and the horses were down at the slough now, getting a thorough cleanup. A half hour later the two families met at the table. Liesbet's brothers, Bruno and Menno, were big and red-faced and silent. Secretly Cornelia hoped that she would not have to marry either of them. When you came to think of it, Schapansky wasn't the most pleasant sounding name in any case.

It was not a decision that had to be made today. But learning to become a housekeeper could not be postponed. She had learned many things this last year. This spring and summer both her mother and grandmother began teaching her in earnest.

The summer was another disappointment. The grasshoppers were not as bad as last year. But they were bad enough. The crop was light, very light. All through the settlement.

Peter Harms cut his acres by scythe, of course. Cornelia and her mother followed, gathering handfuls of the sparse heads, and tying them in bundles with a few

193

stalks of straw. Johann came after, building stooks of the bundles. When the stooks were sufficiently dry, they were taken home by wagon, and spread on a bare, level spot.

The threshing implements were flails—a long stick and a short one joined by a leather thong. Father, Mother, Johann—each had a flail. They worked steadily, raising the sticks above their heads, and bringing them down on the dry sheaves. After a few hours of beating the heads, the sheaves were turned. And again the flail went to work. *Up-Down-Thwack! Up-Down-Thwack!*

Finally, when they were reasonably sure that the grain heads were empty of kernels, the straw was lifted off by forkfuls, and stacked for later use. Brooms, made of brush, were used to sweep what was left into a pile. It looked pitifully small. But even that would be reduced. There was a lot of chaff mixed with the grain, and this would have to be winnowed away.

On a windy day Father and Johann did the winnowing. They tossed shovelfuls of the grain into the air. The chaff blew away. The grain fell to the ground. Slowly, slowly the grain was cleared of chaff. Then it could be stored.

The storage room in the cellar held a few bushels of potatoes and carrots, and several chewed heads of cabbage. It was all the grasshoppers had left them.

"It is something," said Mother with a sigh.

"It is much. Compared to last year, it is much," said Grandmother Siemens.

She did not often speak so vigorously nowadays. Grandmother was getting old. This summer had seen her getting thinner and weaker. Mother had begun to say things like, "Mother, you mustn't lift that. Why don't you go to the Big Room to sit down?"

"What should I do there? Twiddle my thumbs and toes? No, no. No, no. I would rather wear out than rust out."

She perked up—and so did the whole settlement—when the news came that the *Oberschulze* had arrived in Canada with his family. *Now* things would be run the way they ought to be run. Now people would know where to go for good advice when there was disagreement. Teacher Harms had the honored privilege of driving to the landing to meet the Penners when their river steamer docked there. He had borrowed Lanky and Scott for the occasion. Daniel Martens waited there too, to load the Penner boxes and crates onto a wagon. Buggy and wagon drove past the Schanz shelters and directly out to the Harms homestead. This was to be the Penners' home until they built their own.

The Penners had six children, all boys except the youngest, Matilda. She was born after the Harmses left Schoenthal in Russia. So the whole Harms family spilled out to welcome their guests. Cornelia could not sort the Penner boys by name, except Nickolai, of course. Being the oldest he had changed the least. But he had become very, very good-looking. He was still the same tease, though.

When Daniel Martens drove up, Cornelia heard a soft exclamation. "Well! The pigpen boy!"

She didn't think any of the grownups had heard. But Daniel had. His face reddened as if someone had flicked it with a whip.

He was sixteen now, and he looked several years older. For two years he had been doing a man's work. He was Abram Thielmann's right hand man. He certainly did not look much like the castaway boy who huddled, sobbing, under the dripping eaves on the morning when the Harmses left Schoenthal. Yesterday he had come to help butcher a calf, so there would be meat to serve to the important guests. He had stayed particularly to greet the *Oberschulze* and to pay his respects. The great man, and all the grownups, stood in the autumn sunshine, gabbling away. Suddenly the *Oberschulze* turned to Daniel.

"Is this—can this—do you mean to say *this* is *Daniel*? Daniel Martens of Schoenthal?"

"Daniel Martens—the pigpen boy," said Daniel with a hard laugh.

"That is a thing to be forgotten," said Teacher Harms mildly.

"But if people will keep reminding one, what then?" He did not glance at Nickolai.

"Those who do," said the *Oberschulze*, "are not worth listening to."

"No, no. No, no" said Grandmother Siemens. "Now come in, come in, everybody. And tell us things about Russia, our beloved old home."

For the first time she sounded wistful and lonesome.

But Penner was full most of all of the fact that the mass migration had been accomplished. The last Bergthalers had been transferred to Canada. Three thousand people safely transported across a wide ocean and into a strange and new land. They had dreamed of it. They had planned for it. They had lived to see it done. In spite of many hardships they had seen it done.

All told there were about eighteen thousand Mennonites who were part of the migration wave from Russia to the new world—to Kansas, Nebraska, the Dakotas, and Manitoba. They came from every Mennonite colony in Russia. But the Bergthaler colony was the only one that migrated in a body, though in three stages. And much of the responsibility had rested on the shoulders of this man, Oberschulze Penner. The Harms womenfolk felt highly honored to have him as their guest. It was almost like having Moses come to sit at their table.

After supper the two families gathered in the Big Room, where a coal oil lamp held back the night. But Cornelia chose a stool in a shadowy corner. Stories would be told. And they were best enjoyed when there was no one watching her. Nickolai Penner, with his handsome teasing face, for instance. Or Daniel Martens glowering at Nickolai. Silly boys.

The elders compared notes about their journey. The starts and stops. The trains and ships. The storms at sea.

After that the greater part of the conversation had to do with Canada. The things that had happened here—the deaths, the births, the villages that had been founded. The *Oberschulze* was eager to hear it all in detail. The villages that had disbanded and why. The settlers that had crossed the river to *"Jant Sied"*—the other side—to take up new locations. The prospects for the future. The progress that had been made in spite of the grasshoppers. Conditions were so much improved that almost every household had a pig or two to butcher this fall. That was worth a great deal.

A month later cold weather had set in and pig-butchering was in full swing. The Harmses did not get asked to many places. Every one knew that Teacher Harms was tied to his school work. He could not take a man's place at the job. But the Abram Thielmanns asked particularly that Grandmother Siemens, Sarah and Cornelia Harms should come to their *"Schwienstchast"*— "pig wedding"

They were butchering two pigs. That usually meant a long, hard day's work for four couples.

Except for some studying, which she did under her father's direction at home now, Cornelia was done with school. At fourteen and a half years of age she was entering the grownup world. Part of her responsibility this day was keeping two-year-old Sarah-Cornelia out from under everybody's feet. She would have liked to spend the entire day telling stories, reciting nursery rhymes, and singing children's songs to the delight of the child. But that would not do. The Thielmanns were short-handed.

She helped rip the warm and greasy intestines from their web of fat. When that job was done and two women went out to the barnyard to empty the casings (intestines), Cornelia stood by with a pailful of warm water. It was a sunny day, but cold. All three were wrapped in shawls and sweaters. When the casings had been stripped empty—and that was not the most pleasant job—the women turned one end of the casing inside-out, forming a little pocket. It was Cornelia's job to pour warm water into the pocket. One woman shook the pocket. The other fed more casing into it—and Cornelia poured water. Now the whole length was racing through that opening, turning itself inside-out. It was fascinating to watch.

It would be the women's job next to rinse the casings well, and then scrape them with dull knives on a board. After that came the scrubbings, repeated scrubbings, with bran and soap powder, until the casings were pronounced clean. Then more rinsings. Then they were dropped into a panful of salt to wait until they would be needed to make sausage. All of this would take much time and work.

Racing toward the house now, Cornelia glanced in at the partly opened barn door. The men, bulky in overalls and sweaters, were working at a long trestle table. One end was heaped with large hams. The men were cutting slabs of fat off the flanks of the carcass to be made into cracklings. Two men were standing over a tub, scraping hair off a pig's head. It wasn't a pleasant sight now. But just wait till the liversausage and headcheese were done! There was a lot of good eating in a pig's head.

No one glanced up as she ran past, blowing on her red fingers. Daniel wasn't there. He didn't come in for dinner. No one so much as mentioned the boy until mid-afternoon.

Two tables crowded the kitchen. At one, men were stuffing sausages. At the other Cornelia and her Grandmother were busy doing the most tiresome job of all. They were cutting the slabs of fat into tiny, tiny cubes. Thousands and thousands of cubes. Grandmother sat at a corner of the table. But Cornelia stooped over the cutting board. Her neck felt as if it was on fire. There were crawly tingly aches under her shoulder blades. Her fingers were numb from the constant crunch-crunch of the big knife cutting through the fat. But one didn't dare stop. They were working one man short, so everything was late today. It was high time for the cracklings to go into the big cooker. That was a three-in-one job. When cracklings browned, fat oozed out—and there was the lard. At the same time the spareribs would be cooking along with the cracklings.

The kitchen was growing dark. Little Sarah was cranky. Her mother had laid a chair on its side in the doorway so the baby was shut out of the kitchen, though she could watch everybody. That wasn't to her liking at all. Her complaints became sobs.

199

"Suschki, Kruschki, be quiet, be quiet!" pleaded Cornelia. And she began singing one of the baby's favorite songs, about barefoot geese in the straw. It was no use. The baby's cries became screams.

"Wash your hands, quick!" commanded Grandmother. "Go to the child."

Cornelia had picked up the toddler, and was wiping her eyes and nose, when Huldah Thielmann entered from the passage that led to the barn.

"Abram says maybe you people had better go home right away," she called out. "A bad storm is beginning."

As one, everyone turned to the window. Thick swirls of white were sweeping westward.

"You think it's really serious?" said one of the sausage makers.

"Abram says this is only the beginning."

It seemed unbelievable. A short while ago the sun had been shining. Cornelia glanced at the clock. Half past four. Half an hour ago her father and brothers had looked in on their way home from school. Father was to come for the womenfolk after the chores were done at home. Half an hour. Was that long enough for them to have reached home in safety?

"I hope Peter is not on the way," Cornelia heard her mother saying anxiously.

Abram Thielmann entered from the barn. "*Lied* (people), I'm afraid it's almost too late for you to go home. And I'm afraid that this means you'll have to stay here for night."

They discussed it back and forth. There were children at home, waiting for their parents. Only a few doors down, in this village! Yet no one cared to step into the howling whiteness.

"What about Daniel?" said Huldah.

"I can only hope," said her husband, "that he will have the sense to stop at a farm somewhere along the way. I can only hope."

"What if there is no place?"

Daniel had gone to the forest five days ago, and had said he planned to be back tonight. Daniel. Out in this storm. Cornelia hugged Suschki close, and she was remembering another stormy night when the baby was born, and Abram Thielmann almost lost his life.

"He's a sensible boy," said one of the sausage makers.

"Yes, who would have thought that the pigpen boy would ever become so *gescheit*?" (Sensible)

"It's time everyone forgot that nickname," said Abram Thielmann curtly.

"Na, na, I was only making fun. There is no harm in that."

"There is if it hurts someone. Was it Daniel's fault that his own mother wished him dead? And that his second foster mother cast him off? I tell you, it takes a *man* to tread a past like that under his feet. And Daniel is doing it. It's time the people of this village helped him a little."

The helpers dropped the subject, and got on with the work of sausage making.

By now the women were stirring and stirring the sizzling cracklings. Baby Suschki in her arms, Cornelia watched the long wooden paddle go backward and forward, round and round, in the deep iron cooker that hung over a low coal fire. Chunks of spareribs kept bobbing up. Steam rose from the cooker. It gushed from the large kettle on the stove top, where liver sausage was boiling. The kitchen was so full of steam, the two lamps looked timid and sulky.

Hardly anyone spoke. Every few minutes Abram Thielmann went to the door and stuck his head out, straining to hear a sound. Fine snow sifted into the entry. The door groaned each time he closed it. At the third time, Huldah lit two more lamps,and set them on the windows sills. Nobody asked her why.

Little Suschki's head had grown heavier and heavier. It slumped against Cornelia's shoulders now, and she knew the baby must be asleep. She did not lay the child down. It was comforting to hold the soft warm body close. She carried Suschki into the Big Room where Grandmother sat rocking softly. Cornelia heard a whisper. Grandmother was talking—but not to Cornelia. She must be praying for Daniel. Probably Father too. Cornelia felt a band of ice squeezing her heart. What if one were out in this weather? Who could survive it?

That was a strange, restless night. As long as there was work to do, the grownups kept busy. They were glad for each job they could find to do. But finally the last cracklings had been drained. And the last chunks of spareribs packed into crocks and covered with warm lard, so they would remain fresh tasting. The sausages hung over staves in the smoking area above the kitchen. The walls and furniture had been washed down, the floors scrubbed.

A pot of *prips* was near boiling point all night long. The women lay down where they could. The restless men paced the floor, and talked in low muttering voices, and smoked their pipes or cigarets. Cornelia who was curled up on a comforter on the Big Room floor, was bothered most by the smoke. Her eyes stung. Breathing was difficult. Most Bergthaler smoked. Father did not.

When Cornelia awoke, grey light was seeping into the

Big Room. Grandmother and Mother must have changed places during the night. Grandmother had been on the rocker, Mother on the settee. Both were asleep.

Cornelia heard the outer door squeak and groan. She heard whispers. She rolled out of the comforter and padded into the kitchen in her stockings. Huldah Thielmann and her husband were facing one another. "One ox has come home," he was saying.

One ox. One ox. It was like a dull gong sounding in Cornelia's head. There could be no doubt. Something serious had happened to Daniel.

As soon as full daylight had come, the men went outdoors. The storm had spent itself. Everywhere you looked you could see tumbled drifts of snow piled in unexpected places. Not waiting for breakfast, Abram Thielmann hitched a team of horses to a sleigh. He and the men went out to break a trail through the heaped snow. In about two hours the men were back to take the women to their own homes.

Shortly afterwards, Teacher Harms and Ronald Ross arrived. There was no thought of opening school today. Men began to arrive, in sleighs and on foot. Huldah served cups of *prips* and bread with slices of sparerib or liversausage to all who were hungry. *Oberschulze* took a slice from the plate Cornelia held to him.

"You look pale," he said kindly. "Don't give. up hope. We may find Daniel unharmed."

There was a knot in her throat. Father was safe. But Daniel was like a brother. He was Bernhard's best friend.

In the Big Room *Oberschulze* Penner called the men to order. Then, briefly, they planned who would go where in their search.

"We'll find him, all right," Cornelia heard one man mutter. "In spring, when the snow goes."

The last clumping pair of boots tramped out. In groups of four or five the men got into waiting bobsleighs. Horses snorted. Runners squeaked. Trace chains jingled. Then the sounds died away.

All that day and all the next the men of Schoenfeld searched for the boy. The second ox turned up near a stack in a neighboring village. Its nose and ears were frozen, but otherwise it was sound and undamaged. The sleigh was found, too, three miles from Schoenfeld. There was no trace of Daniel.

In the Harms household it seemed almost as if Bernhard had died all over again. They coupled the two names tenderly. They remembered Daniel's sorrow when he heard of Bernhard's death. They remembered his pride when he showed them the heap of logs that was waiting to go into this home of theirs. They remembered how he saved the life of Peter Harms. How much they owed him!

On the evening of the fifth day after the storm Cornelia heard the jingle of trace chains. An open cutter drawn by two frisky horses glided to a stop before the Harms door. Father had stepped outdoors.

"You are Peter Harms?" began the stranger. "I have brought—"

But no one listened to the rest of the sentence. Daniel Martens sat beside the *Englaender* driver.

He stumbled a bit as he walked to the door. His feet were wrapped in cloths, nothing more. His nose and ears and cheeks were swollen, and badly blistered. He looked dreadful—and he looked wonderful. The family escorted him indoors. Grandmother kept exclaiming softly, *"Ne, oba! Ne, oba!"* ("Well! Well!")

Daniel told his story, mumbling the words through his swollen lips. How the storm overtook him. How he decided to set the oxen free. How he dug a narrow trench in a drift and lay down. How he lay face down, with his arms crossed, so he'd have breathing space. How in a minute he was completely covered. How it was a relief to be out of the stinging wind.

But then he faced a new problem. In a short while he was uncomfortably hot. Snow melted. It soaked his pant legs and his jacket. When the wind died down, he broke through the covering of snow. The night, having turned bitterly cold, immediately stiffened his clothes. That was when he began a stumbling run. He had to keep jogging, to keep moving, though he fell again and again, losing all sense of direction. He would have frozen to death if he had not seen the gleam of light. A glimmer, but it saved his life.

He could remember groping for a door. He couldn't remember if he knocked. The first thing he did know clearly was that someone was cutting his stiffly frozen clothes off his body. And someone was patting turpentine all over his face and ears. Soon he was rocking with agony as his feet thawed. But they were going to be all right, he thought, though they were still very tender and covered with purple blisters.

While telling his story, Daniel's glance went slowly all around the room. It lingered on each face in it. Peter Harms's hand went to the boy's shoulder. He squeezed it affectionately.

Sarah Harms handed the boy a cup of *prips*. "Drink. This will warm you up," she said. But her look and action said more than her lips. *Welcome home, Daniel*, they said.

X
And Afterwards

Spring came and Cornelia turned fifteen. That day Grandfather Siemens' seachest was opened.

"Now you are almost a young lady. Choose a gift for yourself," said Grandmother.

There, on top of all the finery—the fancy brocades and the fringed embroidered shawls—lay the old doll, just where the hands of Cornelia had laid it four springs ago. Kneeling before the chest, Cornelia picked up the battered thing. She smiled soberly. Four years. So long ago. That was the day, she remembered now, when she found out that Mother was her stepmother in reality.

"Why stop to look at that useless thing?" exclaimed Grandmother impatiently.

Cornelia's smile widened as she looked up into the wrinkled face. Grandmother's voice still had some snap to it, though it was not as strong as it used to be. "Throw that away, child. Throw that away!"

"*You* didn't," said Cornelia.

"I was foolish. A foolish old woman, who longed for a sight of her *Liebling*. That was the only *Andenken* (remembrance) I had of her."

Cornelia laid the doll aside with a fond pat. As on that day in Steinfeld, Molotschna colony, Russia, she lifted out shawls and trinkets. They were beautiful, but a Mennonite girl could never wear them.

"Well? Well? What is it you would like to have? What are you looking for?"

"The ivory fan. Is that still here?"

"Is that what you would like best? Ach, too bad, too bad. That was my farewell gift to Martha. I felt I would never see her again—and she is my granddaughter after all. She liked the fan best of all, too."

Grandmother was launched on a story now, telling about the gifts she had given Martha's brothers and to Aunt Gerda. Cornelia only half listened. Kneeling there, she studied Grandmother's face, wrinkle by wrinkle. Ever since the day Grandmother made her important choice four years ago, what had she not been to them all! She had come with them to this new country. Through everything she had kept up not only her spirits, but the spirits and courage of all of them. Or so it seemed to Cornelia. When Bernhard died . . . When they spent that dark and damp winter in the *simlin* . . . . When the house was built here, and the cracks had to be caulked . . . When the half rotted sods needed to be chopped fine, so garden vegetables could be seeded . . . When the grasshoppers ate up the young crop . . . Always and always it was Grandmother who heartened everybody else.

Cornelia rose and closed the chest. She went to give Grandmother a hug.

"Well, what now!" exclaimed Grandmother.

"I don't need any birthday present. Ever since we came to Manitoba, do you know who has been our present, on birthdays and everyday? You, Grandmother."

"Ach, such foolishness you talk, child!" protested Grandmother. But two happy tears trickled down her seamy cheeks.

Spring became summer. This summer of 1877 was richly fruitful. In the East Reserve every home was surrounded by beds of bright flowers. Rows of healthy young saplings surrounded each yard. In the neat gardens vegetables were flourishing. Seven hundred families were clustered in thirty-eight villages. Five thousand acres of land were under cultivation. Often now, buggy loads of *Englaender* sightseers would come from Winnipeg to drive gaily through the villages, to stare at the new settlers, to watch them at work. The "Winnipeg Free Press" praised the Mennonites. They were the best settlers that had ever come to Manitoba, the paper said. Daniel Martens read the report in the city, and brought a copy for Teacher Harms to see.

But a greater honour was in store for the settlement. That summer the news came that the Governor General of Canada, Lord Dufferin, meant to visit the East Reserve to see this interesting people for himself.

This news concerned the whole settlement. It concerned Mr. Hespeler, because he had helped to bring the Mennonites from Russia and settle them here. He hurried down from Winnipeg. There were meetings to plan what should be done to do honour to the Governor General. Imagine! The personal representative of Queen Victoria herself! He wanted to assure himself that all was well with them.

There was to be a grand gathering of all who were neither too old nor too young to leave home. A flat-topped rise was chosen as the meeting place. From the summit you could see twelve comfortable villages. There would, of course, be speeches, in German—with Mr. Hespeler to interpret them. There would be songs—with Teacher Harms leading them. His school had been chosen for the honour. Besides this, young girls of the settlement, all dressed in white, would hand bouquets of

208

garden flowers to each lady who travelled with the Governor General's party. Cornelia was one of the girls chosen for this very special honour.

"And then you think I will stay at home?" exclaimed Grandmother Siemens that morning. "No, no. No, no. Such a big *Fest* (festival) I cannot miss."

"But, Mother!" protested Sarah Harms. "You might get chilled."

"It's summer, child. August! What are you *thinking*?"

"It will be a long day, not over until evening. And August evenings in Canada can be chilly. Maybe you are forgetting that," said Sarah firmly.

"Ach, you don't have to coddle me. I am no little chick, still wet from the shell."

So Grandmother rode out in state in the buggy, drawn by the Ross team. She took her place among old friends on the plank benches that had been prepared for them. The sun was hot, but she enjoyed the whole day. The most exciting part, perhaps, was when fifty young men on horseback went riding out to meet the Vice-Regal party. That was to come on horseback too.

Long ago the Mennonites had become good judges of horses. There were handsome horses in the cavalcade. The whole mass of people watched with laughing interest as the fifty riders set off, their horses cutting fancy figures as they tossed their manes and snorted. The boys shouted, waving their hats as they thundered over the knoll and out of sight.

The crowd waited, patiently yet expectantly. Now . . . now . . . . . You could hear voices and the jingle of bridles and the thud of hooves.

"Now they come." The words were like a sigh running through the waiting crowd.

The visitors came in a knot, looking very fashionable and lively and interested. The Mennonite guard of honour had gone wild. They kept racing round and round the visitors in a wide circle, a dizzy whirl.

That was how the great day began. Someone had erected an arbour on top of the rise and covered it with spruce boughs so the visitors could sit comfortably in the shade. The word *WILLKOMMEN* (Welcome) was spelled out in big letters.

Of course the Mennonites sang favorite German hymns of praise and thanksgiving to God for leading them to their new homes. There were speeches of thanks to the Canadian government, too, for welcoming them. The visitors smiled and applauded when the children sang. They smiled again, the ladies especially, when the girls in white came to hand over their bouquets. Some said a few words in German.

Lord Dufferin's speech was long and flattering. Grandmother, who took it all in with a smile, was heard muttering, "Not so flowery, not so flowery, Herr Dufferin. We are people, only people. Without God's help we could have done nothing." But she smiled at the man who seemed to love her people so greatly.

Night had come before the Harmses got home that day. The chores needed to be done. Cows were bawling, pigs squealing. Chickens had gone to roost. By lantern light Cornelia and her father milked the three cows. Sarah Harms hurried to prepare supper for her hungry family. No one noticed that Grandmother, still wearing her shawl, had dropped onto the stone step before the front entry of the house.

"So. Now everything is ready," said Sarah Harms briskly just as the family collected in the kitchen.

"Cornelia, run and call your grandmother."

"Where is she?"

"I think she went to lie down."

But Cornelia was back in a moment, looking startled. "She is not in our room."

"Will she be in the Big Room then?"

No, she was not there, either. The family scattered for a quick search. It was Anton who found the motionless form on the stone step.

He touched it. There was no response. He raced back into the kitchen.

"I found her!" he shouted. "But—but she—she doesn't *move*."

By lamplight she looked asleep. When the light flashed on her face the eyes opened in a puzzled way, and she tottered to her feet. Supported by her daughter and son-in-law she walked waveringly into the kitchen.

"Ach, how tired I am," she remarked. "That work is something I must not try again."

"What work?"

"How can you ask what work? Plastering the house with mud, of course. Look at my hands. Look at the mud!" The hands were clean, but Grandmother's horrified glance went to the lap of her best Sunday black. "Oh, what stupidity! Sarah, Sarah, how could you let me wear this dress while plastering the walls with mud?"

"We'll know better next time, Mother," said Sarah gently. "Now come and have your supper. You have had a long, tiring day."

"Yes. A long, tiring day . . . . . ." The voice trailed away.

Anton, who was staring at his grandmother, whispered, "She's gone to sleep again!"

211

"Catch her!" said Sarah Harms.

Peter jumped to Grandmother's side just in time to save her from toppling off the chair. Over the bowed head, husband and wife exchanged a long anxious look.

"Johann," said Father then, "help me move grandmother to the Corner Room. We'll set the chair on the rug, so. Now pull at the rug . . . And then you or I will have to ride to Schoenfeld to find Daniel. See if he will ride for a doctor."

"Where to?"

"To Winnipeg."

Cornelia, a knot in her throat, touched her father's sleeve. "What is it? What is wrong with Grandmother?

"A stroke, I think."

They put her to bed, where she lay breathing noisily. How could a thing like this happen so suddenly?

Mother roused herself. "Supper waits. Yes, you had better eat, all of you. Try, at least. We'll need strength—to take care of Grandmother."

So for Grandmother's sake they tried to eat. Sarah Harms had cooked milk soup with tiny bits of dough in it. Johann took one mouthful and left the table.

"Where are you going, boy?" called Father.

"To look for Daniel," said the boy in a blurred voice. He disappeared into the passage to the barn. One by one the other spoons were laid down, too. Mother sighed, and began clearing the table.

Daniel must have ridden hard all night. By mid-afternoon he was back bringing an *Englaender* doctor with him. But the man could do nothing to help. Grandmother Siemens had had a stroke, he said. She might get well, she might not. If not, she might die suddenly or she might linger for a while. So they knew exactly as much as they had known before.

She lingered until mid-November. Sometimes her mind was almost clear. Sometimes it wandered. Sometimes she knew no one. And every day they could see she was slipping just a bit farther away from them all. She died on a chilly Wednesday afternoon.

Kind neighbors came to help prepare her body for burial. They brought food. They sang hymns. They talked about what a good woman Grandmother Siemens had been, and how everyone loved her. Along with the sharp sadness, the family felt a tender pride in her.

Toward evening Father took out his writing material and prepared to write a funeral letter. In his beautiful script he began, "It has pleased the Lord of life and death to call to Himself the soul of his child, Katharina (Stobbe) Siemens . . . ."

The letter told who her parents were. It told where she was born and when. It said whom she married and when, and when her husband died. It told how many children she had had, and how many had died. It mentioned her coming to Canada, and when. And it told about her death, and when and where the funeral was to be. Just as on a wedding invitation, a list of names followed. These families were invited to the funeral. Anyone who received the letter was asked to carry it to the home that was next on the list.

Last of all, Cornelia's father took a ruler and inked a broad black border around the letter. When it had dried sufficiently he folded the sheet. Daniel was waiting to start the letter on its rounds.

"What about tonight?" he asked.

"Tonight?" Father looked up blankly.

"Today is Wednesday. Should I tell the Thielmanns to tell the others not to come?"

Wednesday. Each week, now that the fieldwork was done, Wednesday night was the time when the Bible class met in the home here.

"What do you say, Sarah?"

Not for the first time, Sarah Harms surprised her whole family. "I am thinking, What would Mother say? I think she would say, Have it. Do not call it off. This matter concerns eternity."

Her answer pleased Peter Harms deeply. He and his two boys prepared seats as usual. They brought in blocks of firewood and laid planks across them. And the people came. They filled the Big Room and the Middle Room. Tonight there was a gentle hush over the whole group. They sang songs about heaven, smiling and weeping at the same time. And Teacher Harms's talk was about heaven too—and how one can be sure he is going there.

"Not because of our good works," he pointed out. "But because Jesus died so that we may live forever."

Huldah Thielmann spoke up. "I remember the day when I got this assurance. Grandmother Siemens was in my home, along with Sarah and Cornelia. I remember it well. All I knew until then was hoping, and a trembling fear. I can still hear Sarah Harms speak the words, 'There is a knowing. There is a knowing.' That day I left fear behind. I know that I have passed from death into life eternal. Because God's Word says so. Because Jesus died for all my sin. Because I have trusted myself to His keeping."

In the silence that followed, a husky voice came from a shadowy corner of the Big Room. "I—I,too, would like to have this knowing." It was Daniel Martens!

214

"There is a knowing . . . There is a knowing . . ."

The grandfather clock ticked out the words endlessly that night. On her bed on the Big Room floor, Cornelia tossed restlessly from side to side. The Corner Room that she and Grandmother used to share was cold and dark tonight. The body in its white shroud lay stiffly, with folded hands, on a board that was supported by two chairs. A window had been raised slightly so the cold air could enter freely.

Grandmother was—dead? Cornelia couldn't believe it. And neither did her parents or the friends who had gathered here this evening. They believed she was more alive than ever. She was seeing Jesus.

"Bernhard . . . . Grandmother . . . . How can one be sure?" Cornelia asked of the night.

There is a knowing . . . . There is a knowing . . . answered the clock.

She thought of the quiet joy on Daniel's face tonight, and she envied him.

Cornelia awoke to a chilly, rainy morning. She could hear her mother saying anxiously, "Do you have to go, Peter?"

"This is pig-butchering time, as you know. It is hard to find men who are not too busy to dig a grave."

"But you have a chest cold already. Come, let me at least rub some Green Drops on your chest. And make sure you wear the sheepskin coat."

Afterwards people said what a pity it was that Peter Harms ventured out to do the job that day. A foolish thing, altogether. Especially with a chest cold. He never had been strong, they said. His wife should have known better than to allow it. Were there not men enough in the settlement to take over a job like that?

But there were ten persons in Schoenfeld who never asked those questions. They were the ones whom Teacher Harms and Daniel had asked for help in digging the grave. All had had more important things to do that day. At least, they thought at the time that they were more important. As Teacher Harms made his requests very gently, almost apologetically, it was easy to say no to him. Daniel Martens practically pleaded with men to come and help. But who paid much attention to Daniel Martens? Who, except Oberschulze Penner and Abram Thielmann. And both those men happened to be away from home that day. So Daniel and Teacher Harms worked out in the cold slicing rain until the job was finished. Grandmother's funeral need not be postponed.

Immediately after the funeral, when the last funeral guest had eaten the last funeral bun and gone home, Peter Harms went to bed with severe chest pains. Two days later he died.

Father is dead. It was Cornelia's first thought every morning. Each time it was like a new shock, completely unreal and horrible.

She seemed to have broken into several pieces. One part of her was numb, frozen. Part of her moved, and answered questions, and worked, and—sometimes—swallowed food. But her other self, her real self, was like a lost child groping its way through a dark tunnel where no light ever shines. Nothing but bewilderment and pain were there.

Mother and the boys all cried a lot. Johann in the barn, with his face against the harness where Father hung it last. Anton when he started out to school again where a new teacher waited for him. Mother any time of day, but most of all at night. Cornelia would grope her way to the

Middle Room and lie down and put her arms around Mother's shaking shoulders. But she herself couldn't cry.

Her mother worried about it, just as she had when Bernhard died.

"Won't you write a letter to Agatha?" she coaxed one day.

"Didn't Oberschulze Penner say he would send word?"

"Ach, yes. But Agatha will want to hear everything. All the details. She will want to hear them from her family, especially from her very own sister. Think. If *you* were so far away now!"

So Cornelia got out the writing materials, and sat down at the kitchen table.

"Manitoba, Canada. Dec. 2, 1877

Dear Agatha! By now you will have heard that Father died . . . ."

She stared at the words. Dead. Dead. Father's dead. It was like a wave of seasickness washing over her.

"I can't write," she announced, her voice cracking.

"Try, Cornelia."

She took a fresh grip on her pen. ". . . . Do you remember, Agatha, how I used to make fun of Martha because she thought the earth was flat? Well, it is. It's flat, I tell you. *Flat*. There is no shape. There is nothing beautiful. There is no meaning to anything. Father is dead—and it's not *right* that he should be dead. He was good and gentle and wise. He taught people to love God. But why should I love God if He does horrible things like this? Why? Tell, me why? The very worst thing that can happen has happened . . . ."

The words were coming fast now. Cornelia's pen stabbed the paper. Her breath came in shivering gusts.

Mother, sitting opposite, said, "May I read?"

"There." Cornelia shoved the sheet across the table.

"Ach, my child! My poor child!" whispered Mother. Her face dropped to her folded hands. In the long silence Cornelia could hear heavy drops dripping onto the oilcloth table cover.

She crushed the letter. She went to the stove, opened the door, and tossed the sheet into the glowing coals. "What are you making for supper?" she said in a hard dry voice.

People came to visit the Harmses. Some sat in awkward silence. Some chattered about a hundred things that didn't matter. Some came to weep and to tell how much they had loved Teacher Harms. Whoever they were, and however they acted, they seemed to do good to Sarah Harms. Cornelia served coffee and buns and cookies. She answered when people spoke to her. *But my heart is frozen,* she thought. *As frozen as the creek out there . . . .*

And then it was spring again, and Cornelia turned 16.

Sarah had not remembered what day this was. She asked Cornelia's help in a big and very difficult job that had to be done: to pack away all the clothes and personal effects of Grandmother and Father. They had kept postponing the task. Today they cleaned any spots, and hung the garments out for a good sunning before packing them away in Grandmother's seachest.

"Grandmother opened it a year ago today," said Cornelia in a dreamy voice.

"What did you say?" said Mother absently. Then her eyes sharpened. "Why, Cornelia! It is your *birthday*. How could I forget?"

"It doesn't matter."

"Of course it matters!" said Sarah indignantly. "Such a day for this work! It is a shame."

218

It was too late to change that now. They worked together silently. All Grandmother's fancy gifts from her sailor husband were packed into the bottom drawer of the big wardrobe in the Big Room. Into the chest went the Sunday and "small Sunday"—second best—clothes of Grandmother and Father.

"What about Father's books?" said Cornelia.

"I have been thinking maybe you would like them."

"Oh, may I?" Light flashed across her face as it hadn't in months. "Johann will want the books about machines. And Anton will like the animal books."

"But only my daughter would care for the grammars in Russian and German and English," teased Sarah Harms. "And the geographies, and histories, the stories of many lands. Just one thing worries me. What Mennonite man will want a wife who is wiser than he is?"

Cornelia slid to the floor. Her back, tired from long stooping, rested against the old chest. "If he is any good, he will not mind," she said. "I like books. I can't help it. I am Cornelia Harms, the daughter of Teacher Harms. I can't help it. And I wouldn't want to help it."

"Bernhard was like you in that," said Sarah Harms as she closed and locked the chest. "My own two are Siemenses through and through. Good boys, but not hungry in their minds. Were you going to say something?"

It was not easy for Cornelia to voice the sudden longing that had come to her. "You said something— about my birthday—There is one thing I would like to have."

"What is that?"

"One day. A day to go—alone—to visit Bernhard's grave. May I?"

219

"Of course. Tomorrow?"

"Oh, may I?" She hadn't thought permission would be given so easily.

She had expected to walk, if she went at all. It was only five miles to go. But Sarah Harms thought she had better borrow the Ross horses if they were free. *Then I'll go to the landing too*, thought Cornelia. *I'll go to all the places where we went together, Bernhard and I.*

He had seemed so grownup and wise, and so patient with his quicksilver sister. It was strange to think that she was two years older now than he was when he died.

Mother thought of coming with her. She practically offered to come. Cornelia did not encourage the thought. She had a special reason why she did not want Mother's company on that special tomorrow.

With the coming of spring a new cloud of trouble had arisen in Cornelia's sky. It was a black cloud that was rapidly growing and threatened to blot out every bit of sunlight. She wondered if Johann and Anton were aware of the threat. She never mentioned the thing to them. Nor to her mother of course. After all, Mother was the centre of the entire problem.

Solomon Schultz meant to marry Sarah Harms. That was the bald fact—as plain and unattractive as the nose on his face. His own wife, his second one, had died at Christmastime, a month after the death of Teacher Harms. For the past three weeks he had been finding the most amazing reasons to drop in at the Harmses. Already he handed out advice to Johann on how to treat the land. He ventured to boss Anton. He asked Sarah's advice on how to set broody hens. He pinched Cornelia's cheek. Once. After that she made sure he never got within pinching range.

He might not be a bad man. His second wife was the one who whipped Lena so unmercifully and almost starved her, and taught her own children to scorn her. But Solomon Schultz *let* her do these wicked things. And it wasn't that he was a meek man. Cornelia had no use for him. And last Sunday he brought his entire family for an afternoon visit. The children snatched food. They were *grotmulig* (big mouthed) to Lena, and made her life a misery. What if Mother became Mrs. Solomon Schultz the third? What if the two households had to live together always? Cornelia knew of several "brought-together" families. Most of these arrangements seemed to work out fairly well. Some very well. But—

One good thing had come out of the trouble. Cornelia had begun to pray again. *Don't let it happen, Lord. Please, don't let it happen.* If Mother married Mr. Schultz, that would be worse than Father's death.

For months Cornelia had been bitter toward God. She felt guilty now about praying. What right did she have to come to God and ask for *anything*? But Jesus said, "Come unto me all ye that are heavy laden . . . ." She was. She needed help, and she needed it fast. Who else was there for her to turn to?

She leaned her dark head against the warm and silky flank of Brindle that evening. Moodily she watched the milk go frothing into the pail. Johann passed and repassed her with forkloads of oatsheaves. Suddenly he grounded his fork beside her, and leaned on it.

"*You* talk to her!" he blurted.

She looked up startled. "To whom? About what?"

"To Mother, of course," he said impatiently. "About that—that—. Cornelia, if that man comes here to live, I'll run away. I won't stay home one single day. I tell you, I won't."

221

"You mean Solomon Schultz?"

"Of course! Who else? You'll talk to her, won't you?"

But now they had come to the heart of Cornelia's trouble. She said, distressed, "But how can I? I'm only her stepdaughter!"

He sniffed scornfully. "Who thinks of that? Anton and I don't. Nor does Mother. So you'll talk to her, won't you?"

If Daniel Martens didn't choose that moment to enter the barn. His coming was nothing unusual. He generally checked in two or three times a week. But in Cornelia's opinion he was entirely too much at home here.

"What are you to talk to your mother about?" he wanted to know.

"Solomon Schultz," said Cornelia shortly.

"Has he been here again? I told him week before last that he had lost nothing here." (That is, "Don't look for anything here.")

Cornelia was surprised into a giggle. "What did he say to that?"

"He said that that was no matter for a pigpen boy to decide. He said only your mother could make that decision—"

"*She has made it.*"

A guilty red flooded the three faces. They swung to look at the inner door. There stood Sarah Harms. She smiled slightly. "Foolish children. Come in to supper. You, too, Daniel—if you like *Rollkuchen* as much as you used to. Today is Cornelia's birthday. Did you know that?"

At the table she announced that Solomon Schultz would not be coming again.

Johann who had spread his tenth cruller with syrup,

222

took a huge bite. "But why didn't you send him packing long ago?"

"Johann! Use more refined language, if you please! Such a thing to say about a grownup!" Then her severity relented. "The children needed a few good meals, unmannerly or not. Lena needed help and encouragement in her hard task. And as for their father— I couldn't give an answer to a question that had not been asked, could I? Boys, boys, behave yourselves! Who are the unmannerly ones now?"

Now that the immense weight had been lifted Cornelia would possibly have changed her mind about tomorrow's trip. But her mother had gone to the bother of asking for the team, and had baked a tart for her lunch. She set off with mixed feelings. Excitement, reluctance, relief. All were part of her that morning.

The landing was almost unchanged. There was the brown, tree-shaded river. There were the Indian tents. There were the barrels and crates, waiting for the next steamer. But by next year all of this might disappear. This very year, 1878, a railway was to be built from Emerson to Winnipeg. It would link Manitoba not only with the railroads in the United States but with eastern Canada as well. But for the time being, things looked as they had four years ago.

For a long while Cornelia stood there dreaming. She saw herself at twelve, landing with Bernhard. New immigrants. She saw other steamers coming in, and she was one of the crowd of watchers when more and more Mennonites landed here. She saw the watchers make way while several plain board coffins were carried down the gangplank.

The Schanz shelters looked neglected, and were

beginning to fall into ruin. It was a place for birds and wild animals to shelter now. She could hear birds rustling and twittering in the rafters. She wasn't even sure which of the derelict buildings was the one in which they stayed, where Bernhard died.

The cemetery looked almost as neglected. There were thirty humps of grass, some with markers, some with none. Bernhard's marker, darkened by the weather, had fallen. She propped it up with rocks. Her fingers traced the letters cut there by Father's hands: Bernhard, beloved son of Peter and Sarah Harms, Born March 29, 1861, in Russia. Died Aug. 30, 1874, in Canada. "Blessed are the dead who die in the Lord."

Blessed. Happy? Yes, Bernhard was happy that day when he slipped away so peacefully. Today Cornelia could look at the words and remember that evening without flinching. She had experienced so much since. She thought of Grandmother, who lived so long, and faded so gradually. But at the end she had been so tired, and one could not really be sorrowful about her death. Father was different. He went so fast. Cornelia bowed her head on her knees and gave way to her grief at last. He went so fast, in such great pain. You wanted to help him breathe, and you couldn't.

"Happy are the dead who die in the Lord . . . ."

There was no one at home when Cornelia got back from her pilgrimage. A note on the kitchen table said they had all gone to Schoenfeld. When she needed them so! When she had so much to tell!

Restlessly she hurried through her chores. Still no sign of them. She made a search of the pantry, and found a few remaining *Rollkuchen*. Cold coffee, a cup of milk, the crullers and syrup were her supper. Then she got out the writing material and began a letter.

Dear Agatha,

I have so much to tell you that I do not know where to begin. I was so unhappy about Grandmother and Father—especially about Father—that I was angry with God. Did Mother write you about that? Oh, I was bitter. I thought, how can I love God if He lets these things happen?—the very worst things that *could* ever happen. But that wasn't true. God let me see that that wasn't true. Agatha, *Solomon Schultz wanted to marry Mother.* Oh, I was afraid! And fear taught me to pray again.

Mother said last night that many of our people will think she did a very foolish thing when she "gave him the basket." (Turned down his proposal.) How can a woman think she is able to farm alone, they will say. But I don't care. I don't care how hard we have to work. It will be worth it.

Mother said something that truly warms my heart. She said that Solomon Schultz is *too small*. She says that she has known and lived with a giant! Agatha, Mr. Schultz weighs about *two* times as much as Father! But I know what she means, and I know you will understand too.

Oh, it is as if a thick cloud has been lifted suddenly, and the sun can shine again. But maybe that is because of what happened today. Agatha, I went to the place where Bernhard is buried. I sat in the grass listening to the wind and the meadowlarks. And to God. For once I was ready to listen to Him. I think He has beeh trying to make me hear for a long, long while.

225

It was like another burial out there in the grass-grown cemetery, but a burial with a resurrection. I don't know—was I the grave-digger, or was God? Both, I think. In partnership. Into the grave went all the bitter feelings of the past months.

They are not dead. Our loved ones are not dead. And now I know that I will not die either. I will see them again.

When I was angry with God—so foolish was I—I said that there was no shape, no meaning to anything. That was wrong. We may not always *see* why God allows things to happen. Not right away. Who would have thought that we would have three graves in four years? And we are not the only ones. We do not know why these things happen. But one day we will.

How are we going to manage the farm? We do not know. There will be many problems. But God will be there. Mother says we need to learn to take grace, one day at a time.

Your loving sister,
Cornelia.

GLOSSARY

Andenken - remembrance (German)
Auf wieder sehen - till we meet again (German)
Dauts gescheit - that's sensible (Low German)
Fest - festival, festive occasion (German)
Fettkuchen - fritters (German)
Fibel - primer (German)
Frisch an's Werk - back to work (German)
Frische Luft - fresh air (German)
Froehliche Weihnachten - Merry Christmas (German)
Gescheit - sensible (German)
Grotmulig - bigmouthed (Low German)
Gruetze - oatmeal porridge (German)
Gruffbrodt - brown bread (Low German)
Heldin - heroine (German)
Jant Sied - the other side (Low German)
Juengling - young man (German)
Keck - pert (German)
Kielke - noodles (Low German)
Liebling - darling (German)
Lied - people (Low German)
Ne oba - well, well (Low German)
Neksch - balky (Low German)
Oberschultze - mayor or reeve (German)
Ohms - preachers (Low German)
Pluma Moos - fruit soup (Low German)
Prips - coffee substitute (Low German)
Rollkuchen - crullers (German)
Schelm - rascal (German)
Schlore - wooden sandals (Low German)
Schnettke - biscuits (Low German)
Schulzenbott - village business meeting (German)
Schwindsucht - consumption, tuberculosis (German)
Schwienstchast - pig wedding (Low German)
Speck - bacon (German)
Streifenfluren - strip farms (German)
Susliki - gopher (Russian)
Upwadasehne - Until we meet again (Low German)

Utstia - dowry (Low German)
Vaspa - midafternoon refreshments (Low German)
Versteck - Hide-and-Seek (German)
Vorsaenger - song leaders (German)
Werst - 1 mile equals 1.5 werst (German)
Willkomen - welcome (German)
Wunsch - verse (German)

Christian Light Publications, Inc., is a nonprofit, conservative Mennonite publishing company providing Christ-centered, Biblical literature including books, Gospel tracts, Sunday school materials, summer Bible school materials, and a full curriculum for Christian day schools and homeschools.

For more information about the ministry of CLP or its publications, or for spiritual help, please contact us at:

Christian Light Publications, Inc.
P. O. Box 1212
Harrisonburg, VA 22803-1212

Telephone—540-434-0768
Fax—540-433-8896
E-mail—info@clp.org